D0032075

DATE DUE

DEC 06 '91			

A P

zpan

PB   7.95
398.2   Uchida, Yoshiko
.Uch   The Magic Listening Cap

MILPITAS UNIFIED SCHOOL DISTRICT
EIA/LEP
Milpitas Unified School District
Milpitas, California
Zanker School

We Deliver Learning

Books by Yoshiko Uchida:

The Dancing Kettle
The Magic Listening Cap
Takao and Grandfather's Sword
The Promised Year
Mik and the Prowler
New Friends for Susan
The Full Circle
Makoto, the Smallest Boy
Rokubei and the Thousand Rice Bowls
The Forever Christmas Tree
Sumi's Prize
Sumi's Special Happening
Sumi and the Goat and the Tokyo Express
The Sea of Gold
In-Between Miya
Hisako's Mysteries
*Journey to Topaz
*Samurai of Gold Hill
The Birthday Visitor
The Rooster Who Understood Japanese
Journey Home
A Jar of Dreams
Desert Exile
The Best Bad Thing
The Happiest Ending
Picture Bride

*published by Creative Arts Book Co.

The Magic Listening Cap
More Folk Tales from Japan

RETOLD AND ILLUSTRATED BY

YOSHIKO UCHIDA

BERKELEY • 1987
CREATIVE ARTS BOOK COMPANY

COPYRIGHT, 1955, BY YOSHIKO UCHIDA
COPYRIGHT RENEWED, 1983, BY YOSHIKO UCHIDA
ILLUSTRATIONS COPYRIGHT, 1987, BY
YOSHIKO UCHIDA

*All rights reserved, including
the right to reproduce this book
or portions thereof in any form.*

This is a new edition of the book
originally published by
Harcourt, Brace and World.

Creative Arts edition published 1987.

For information contact:

Creative Arts Book Company
833 Bancroft Way
Berkeley, California 94710
ISBN 0-88739-016-1
Library of Congress Catalog Card No. 55-5240

PRINTED IN THE UNITED STATES OF AMERICA

For Mabel P. Marshall

PREFACE

I first collected these fourteen folk tales when I was in Japan on a Ford Foundation Fellowship in 1954. When I discovered them, they had already been told and retold to generations of children in Japan.

But they continue to appeal to us even today because they speak of our human condition — of our greed and cruelty, of our kindness and goodness — revealing our weaknesses with humor and warmth.

The universality of folk tales binds people together everywhere — past and present — and in today's fragmented world, I find it cause for rejoicing that there are still books and stories that can help us celebrate our common humanity.

YOSHIKO UCHIDA

Berkeley, California
January 1987

Contents

THE MAGIC LISTENING CAP   3
Adapted from *Kiki Mimi Zukkin*

THE TERRIBLE LEAK   13
Adapted from *Furuya no Mori*

THE WRESTLING MATCH OF THE TWO BUDDHAS   23
Adapted from *Kibutsu Chyoja*

THE MAGIC MORTAR   33
Adapted from *Umi no Mizu wa Naze Karai*

THE TUBMAKER WHO FLEW TO THE SKY   43
Adapted from *Sora ye Nobotta Okeya-san*

THREE TESTS FOR THE PRINCE   53
Adapted from *Nezumi no Tegara*

THE DEER OF FIVE COLORS   65
Adapted from *Go-shiki no Shika*

THE GOLDEN AXE   73
Adapted from *Kogane no Ono*

Contents

THE MOUNTAIN WITCH AND THE PEDDLER   83
Adapted from *Yama Uba to Umakata*

THE MAN WHO BOUGHT A DREAM   93
Adapted from *Yume-kai Chyoja*

THE FOX AND THE BEAR   103
Adapted from *Kitsune to Kuma*

THE TINY GOD   113
Adapted from *Chiisai Kami-sama*

THE RICE CAKE THAT ROLLED AWAY   123
Adapted from *Dango Jyodo*

THE GRATEFUL STORK
Adapted from *Tsuru no On-Gayeshi*   133

THE MAGIC LISTENING CAP

More Folk Tales from Japan

The Magic Listening Cap

There once lived an honest old man who was kind and good, but who was so poor, he hardly had enough to eat each day. What made him sadder than not having enough to eat himself was that he could no longer bring an offering to his guardian god at the nearby shrine.

"If only I could bring even an offering of fish," he thought sadly.

Finally, one day, when his house was empty and he had nothing left to eat, he walked to the shrine of his god. He got on his knees and bowed down before him.

"I've come today to offer the only thing I have left," he said sadly. "I have only myself to offer now. Take my life if you will have it."

The old man knelt silently and waited for the god to speak.

Soon there was a faint rumbling, and the man heard a voice that seemed to come from far, far away.

"Don't worry, old man," the god said to him. "You have been honest and you have been good. From today on I shall change your fortune, and you shall suffer no longer."

Then the guardian god gave the old man a little red cap. "Take this cap, old man," he said. "It is a magic listening cap. With this on your head, you will be able to hear such sounds as you have never heard before."

The old man looked up in surprise. He was old, but he heard quite well, and he had heard many, many sounds during the long years of his life.

"What do you mean?" he asked. "What new sounds are there in this world that I have not yet heard?"

The god smiled. "Have you ever really heard what the nightingale says as it flies to the plum tree in the spring? Have you ever understood what the trees whisper to one another when their leaves rustle in the wind?"

The old man shook his head. He understood.

"Thank you, dear god," he said. "I shall treasure my magic cap forever." And carrying it carefully, he hurried toward his home.

As the old man walked along, the sun grew hot, and he stopped to rest in the shade of a big tree that stood at the roadside. Suddenly, he saw two black crows fly into the tree. One came from the mountains, and the other from the sea. He could hear their noisy chatter fill the air above him. Now was the time to try his magic cap! Quickly, he put it on, and as soon as he did, he could understand everything the crows were saying.

"And how is life in the land beyond the sea?" asked the mountain crow.

"Ah, life is not easy," answered the crow of the sea. "It grows harder and harder to find food for my young ones. But tell me, do you have any interesting news from the mountains?"

"All is not well in our land either," answered the crow from the mountains. "We are worried about our friend, the camphor tree, who grows weaker and weaker, but can neither live nor die."

"Why, how can that be?" asked the crow of the sea.

"It is an interesting tale," answered the mountain crow. "About six years ago, a wealthy man in our town built a guest house in his garden. He cut down the camphor tree in order to build the house, but the roots were never dug out. The tree is not dead, but neither can it live, for each time it sends new shoots out from beneath the house, they are cut off by the gardener."

"Ah, the poor tree," said the crow of the sea sympathetically. "What will it do?"

"It cries and moans constantly, but alas, human beings

5

are very stupid," said the mountain crow. "No one seems to hear it, and it has cast an evil spell on the wealthy man and made him very ill. If they don't dig up the tree and plant it where it can grow, the spell will not be broken and the man will soon die. He has been ill a long time."

The two crows sat in the tree and talked of many things, but the old man who listened below could not forget the story of the dying man and the camphor tree.

"If only I could save them both," he thought. "I am probably the only human being who knows what is making the man ill."

He got up quickly, and all the way home, he tried to think of some way in which he might save the dying man. "I could go to his home and tell him exactly what I heard," he thought. "But surely no one will believe me if I say I heard two crows talking in a tree. I must think of a clever way to be heard and believed."

As he walked along, a good idea suddenly came to him. "I shall go disguised as a fortune teller," he thought. "Then surely they will believe me."

The very next day, the old man took his little red cap, and set out for the town where the sick man lived. He walked by the front gate of this man's home, calling in a loud voice, "Fortunes! Fortunes! I tell fortunes!" Soon the gate flew open and the sick man's wife came rushing out.

"Come in, old man. Come in," she called. "Tell me how I can make my husband well. I have had doctors from near and far, but not one can tell me what to do."

The old man went inside and listened to the woman's story. "We have tried herbs and medicines from many, many lands, but nothing seems to help him," she said sadly.

Then the old man said, "Did you not build a guest house in your garden six years ago?" The wife nodded. "And hasn't your husband been ill ever since?"

"Why, yes," answered the wife, nodding. "That's right. How did you know?"

"A fortune teller knows many things," the old man answered, and then he said, "Let me sleep in your guest house tonight, and by tomorrow I shall be able to tell you how your husband can be cured."

"Yes, of course," the wife answered. "We shall do anything you say."

And so, that night after a sumptuous feast, the old man was taken to the guest house. A beautiful new quilt was laid out for him on the *tatami*, and a charcoal brazier was brought in to keep him warm.

As soon as he was quite alone, the old man put on his little red cap and sat quietly, waiting to hear the camphor tree speak. He slid open the paper doors and looked out at the sky sprinkled with glowing stars. He waited

7

and he waited, but the night was silent and he didn't even hear the whisper of a sound. As he sat in the darkness, the old man began to wonder if the crows had been wrong.

"Perhaps there is no dying camphor tree after all," he thought. And still wearing his red cap, the old man climbed into the quilts and closed his eyes.

Suddenly, he heard a soft rustling sound, like many leaves fluttering in the wind. Then he heard a low gentle voice.

"How do you feel tonight, camphor tree?" the voice called into the silence.

Then the old man heard a hollow sound that seemed to come from beneath the floor.

"Ah, is that you, pine tree?" it asked weakly. "I do not feel well at all. I think I am about to die . . . about to die . . ." it wailed softly.

Soon, another voice whispered, "It's I, the cedar from across the path. Do you feel better tonight, camphor tree?"

And one after the other, the trees of the garden whispered gently to the camphor tree, asking how it felt. Each time, the camphor tree answered weakly, "I am dying . . . I am dying . . ."

The old man knew that if the tree died, the master of the house would also die. Early the next morning, he hur-

8

ried to the bedside of the dying man. He told him about the tree and about the evil spell it had cast upon him.

"If you want to live," he said, "have the camphor tree dug up quickly, and plant it somewhere in your garden where it can grow."

The sick man nodded weakly. "I will do anything, if only I can become well and strong again."

And so, that very morning, carpenters and gardeners were called to come from the village. The carpenters tore out the floor of the guest house and found the stump of the camphor tree. Carefully, carefully, the gardeners lifted it out of the earth and then moved it into the garden where it had room to grow. The old man, wearing his red cap, watched as the tree was planted where the moss was green and moist.

"Ah, at last," he heard the camphor tree sigh. "I can reach up again to the good clean air. I can grow once more!"

As soon as the tree was transplanted, the wealthy man began to grow stronger. Before long, he felt so much better he could get up for a few hours each day. Then he was up all day long, and, finally, he was completely well.

"I must thank the old fortune teller for saving my life," he said, "for if he had not come to tell me about the camphor tree, I would probably not be alive today."

And so he sent for the old man with the little red cap.

"You were far wiser than any of the doctors who came from near and far to see me," he said to the old man. Then, giving him many bags filled with gold, he said, "Take this gift, and with it my life-long thanks. And when this gold is gone, I shall see that you get more."

"Ah, you are indeed very kind," the old man said happily, and taking his gold, he set off for home.

As soon as he got home, he took some of the gold coins and went to the village market. There he bought rice cakes and sweet tangerines and the very best fish he could find. He hurried with them to his guardian god, and placed them before his shrine.

"My fortunes have indeed changed since you gave me this wonderful magic cap," the old man said. "I thank you more than I can say."

Each day after that, the old man went to the shrine, and never forgot to bring an offering of rice or wine or fish to his god. He was able to live in comfort, and never had to worry again about not having enough to eat. And, because he was not a greedy man, he put away his magic listening cap and didn't try to tell any more fortunes. Instead, he lived quietly and happily the rest of his days.

The Terrible Leak

One rainy night, long, long ago, a small boy sat with his grandmother and grandfather around a charcoal brazier. Warming their hands over the glowing coals, they told stories and talked of many things. Outside, the wind blew and the rain splattered on the thatched roof of the cottage.

The old man looked up at the ceiling saying, "I surely hope we don't have a leak. Nothing would be so terrible as to have to put up a new thatched roof now when we are so busy in the fields."

The little boy listened to the lonely wail of the wind as it whipped through the bamboo grove. He shivered, and turned to look at his grandfather's face. It was calm and smiling and unafraid.

"Ojii-san," the little boy said suddenly. "Is there anything you're afraid of?"

The old man laughed. "Why, of course, lad," he said. "There are many things a man fears in life."

"Well then," said the little boy, "what are you *most* afraid of in all the world?"

The old man rubbed his bald head, and thought for a moment as he puffed on his pipe.

"Let me see," he said. "Among human beings, I think I fear a thief the most."

Now, at the very moment the old man was saying this, a thief had climbed onto the roof of the cowshed, hoping to steal one of the cows. He happened to hear what the old man said, and he thrust out his chest proudly.

"So!" he thought to himself. "I am the very thing the old man fears most in all the world!" And he laughed to think how frightened the old man and woman would be if they only knew a thief was in their yard this very minute.

"Ojii-san," the little boy went on. "Of all the animals in the world, which one are you most afraid of?"

Again, the old man thought for a moment, and then he said, "Of all the animals, I think I fear the wolf the most."

Just as the old man said this, a wolf was prowling around the cowshed, for he had come to see if there were some chickens he might steal. When he heard what the old man said, he laughed to himself. "Ah-ha!" he said.

14

"So I am the animal the old man fears the most," and wiggling his nose, he sniffed haughtily.

But inside the house, the little boy went on. "Ojii-san," he said, "even more than a thief or a wolf, what are you the most, most, *most* afraid of?"

The old man sat thinking for a long while, and thoughts of ogres and demons and terrible dragons filled the little boy's head. But the old man was listening to the rain as it splashed and trickled in rivulets of water around the house. He thought again how terrible it would be to have a leak in his roof. He turned to the boy and said, "Well, the one thing I fear most of all right now is a leak! And I'm afraid one may come along any minute!"

Now when the thief and the wolf heard this, they didn't know the old man was talking about a leak in the roof.

"A leak," thought the thief. "What kind of terrible animal could that be? If the old man fears it more than a thief or a wolf, it must be a fearsome thing!"

Down below, the wolf thought the same thing. "A leak must be a dreadful creature if the old man fears it more than me or a thief," he thought. And he peered into the darkness, wondering if a leak might not spring out of the forest, for the old man had said one might come at any moment.

Up on the roof of the cowshed, the thief got so excited he slipped and tumbled down into the darkness. But instead of falling to the ground, he fell right on the back of the wolf.

The wolf gave a frightened yelp. From somewhere above him in the dark night, something had leaped on his back and was clutching his neck. "This must be the terrible leak the old man talked about," thought the wolf, and with his tail between his legs, he ran pell-mell into the woods.

Now the thief did not know he had landed on the back of a wolf. He knew he had fallen on the back of something large and cold and full of fur. What's more, it had given a wild yelp and begun to run. The thief was so frightened he couldn't even call for help. Instead, he clung to the neck of this creature that seemed to be flying through the night into the forest.

"I must be on the back of the terrible leak the old man talked about," he thought fearfully, and closing his eyes tight, he hung on. The harder the thief clung to the wolf's neck, the faster the wolf ran.

As they got deeper and deeper into the forest, branches of trees swung low and scratched the thief's face. Finally, when he felt a big branch sweep past, he caught it and swung himself up into a tree. But the wolf did not know what had happened, and he ran on and on until he came to his cave at the farthest end of the forest. When he finally stopped, he realized the thing on his back was gone.

"Ah, the leak has dropped off somewhere!" he thought, and he sighed a great sigh of relief.

Early the next morning, the wolf went to see his friend, the tiger.

"Mr. Tiger, Mr. Tiger! What a terrible fright I had last night," he said, panting at the very thought of it. "Do you know what kind of creature a leak is?"

The tiger shook his head. "Why, I don't believe I've ever heard of anything called a leak," he said. "What is it?"

"It is something human beings fear more than anything else in this world," said the wolf. "And do you know, one of those terrible creatures jumped on my back last night? I ran all night through the forest with this leak hanging onto my neck, for it clutched at me and almost choked me to death!"

The tiger grunted sympathetically. "Ah, how terrible that must have been," he said.

The wolf took a deep breath and went on.

"The leak dropped off somewhere after I got into the forest, but I'm sure it must still be here. If we don't capture it, none of us will ever be safe again. Will you help me to find it?"

The tiger nodded. "Certainly, I'll help," he said. "Besides, I'd like to see what a leak looks like. I wonder if it has two heads?"

And so the tiger and the wolf set off to look for the terrible leak. As they prowled through the forest, a monkey sitting in a tree peered through the leaves and saw them below.

"Say, Mr. Tiger! Mr. Wolf!" he called. "Where are you going with such worried frowns on your faces?"

"We are searching for a thing called a leak," they answered. "It is something so terrible that human beings fear it more than a thief or a wolf. It must surely be the most fearsome thing in the whole world, and we cannot live safely in this forest until we capture it."

The monkey listened carefully. "A leak?" he asked. "Why, I've never heard of such a creature. Surely, you must be mistaken."

But the wolf shook his head. "No, no! I am not mistaken, for this very creature clutched at my throat and rode on my back all the way into the forest last night. It dropped off somewhere, and must be hiding near us this very minute!"

Now the monkey had seen the wolf running through the forest the night before, with the thief hanging on to his neck. He suddenly realized that this terrible thing they feared was only a human being, so he said in a loud, bragging voice, "Why, if that is the thing you are searching for, I can tell you where he is. He is sitting on one of the branches of the tree over there. In fact, I shall go and capture him single-handed if you want me to."

The tiger and the wolf looked over at the tree where the monkey pointed. Sure enough, there, on one of the branches, sat a creature looking somewhat like a human being. The tiger growled and bared his long, sharp teeth. The wolf looked up at the sky and howled a long, piercing yowl. The thief heard their cries, and trembling with fear, he fell off the branch and went tumbling into a hole in the trunk of the tree.

As the three animals saw him fall, they ran over to the tree and stood around the hole where the thief was hiding.

"Now, how shall we go about capturing this leak?" they said to one another.

"Whoever captures him will become king of the forest," the tiger said. "For he will surely be the bravest and strongest of all."

"That is an excellent idea," said the monkey. Then, because he knew this leak was only a human being who was frightened himself, he marched right up to the hole in the tree trunk. He thrust his tail inside and flipped it about saying, "Are you in there, Mr. Leak? Are you inside?"

The thief had heard the animals as they talked outside

the tree. "It will never do to let them capture me," he thought. "For if they catch me, they will surely kill me."

He decided he must do something to frighten them away, so he grabbed the monkey's tail and pulled as hard as he could. Then, he growled and shouted fiercely, trying to sound more terrible than the tiger and the wolf put together.

"Help!" shouted the monkey as he felt his tail being pulled.

The thief pulled hard, but the monkey pulled even harder, for he didn't want to be dragged into the hole in front of the tiger and the wolf. They both pulled so hard the monkey's tail broke off with a snap, and the monkey went sprawling onto the ground.

"My tail, my tail! My beautiful tail!" he shrieked, and he ran off into the forest, disappearing into the leaves of a tall cedar tree.

"The leak is certainly a fearful thing," said the wolf, shaking his head, and with a great howl he ran off into the woods after the monkey.

"It is best to leave such fearful things alone," said the tiger in a soft voice, and he went slinking off into the woods after the monkey and the wolf.

When all the animals had gone, the thief crept out of the tree trunk. He looked about carefully to make sure that nothing was following him, and then he ran as fast as he could out of the forest.

The thief never learned that what he thought was the terrible leak was only a frightened wolf. And the wolf never discovered that what he thought was the most terrible thing in all the world was only a frightened thief.

And the little boy and his grandmother and grandfather didn't have to be afraid of a leak in the roof after all, for in the stillness of the night the rain stopped, the moon came out bright and clear, and the next days were full of the promise of sunshine.

The Wrestling Match of the Two Buddhas

Once, long ago, there lived a poor but pious man who worked for a wealthy landowner. The one thing the servant wanted more than anything else was to have a statue of Buddha for his own that he might worship each day. Since he was too poor to buy one, he wished instead that he might worship the golden Buddha his master owned. But the master was too busy making money to care about worshiping his Buddha. He kept the golden Buddha locked inside his family altar, and opened it only on special festival days once or twice a year. Then, he would offer the Buddha a few rice cakes or some wine, and murmur a quick prayer.

"If only I could worship the golden Buddha in my own room for even a day," the poor servant thought to himself. But the family altar remained locked, and the servant could not even see the golden Buddha.

One day, when the servant went out to the woods to collect kindling for the fire, he saw a piece of wood lying beside the trunk of a tree. When he looked closely, he saw that it looked exactly like the image of Buddha.

"Why, here is a wooden Buddha I can put up in my altar," thought the servant, and he picked up the piece of wood carefully, brushed off the dirt, and carried it home with him. Then, he put the wooden Buddha in a little altar in his room and worshiped before it each day. He offered a tray of food to his Buddha before each meal, bowing low and saying, "I offer you my humble food. Please take of it what you will." Only after the tray had been in front of the Buddha first did he take the food to eat himself.

Now when the master saw what the servant was doing, he laughed and made fun of him.

"Why, you are worshiping a stick of wood!" he said. "Your Buddha is nothing but the branch of a tree."

Soon the other servants of the household heard about this man, and they came to mock him saying, "He is worshiping a wooden stick! He is worshiping the branch of a tree!" They peered into his room as the servant offered food to his Buddha, and they laughed and called him a fool.

The master realized, however, what a hard-working man this servant was. "I must think of some way to keep him working for me," he thought selfishly. "I will never again be able to find another man who works so hard for so little money." So he tried to think of some way in which he might make the servant stay. At last he had an idea, and he ordered the servant to come before him.

"I have an excellent idea," he said to the servant. "Would you like to watch a wrestling match?"

Now the servant thought this was a very strange thing for the master to ask, but he answered, "Yes, master, I am very fond of wrestling matches."

"Good!" said the master. "I will let you see one more interesting than any you have ever seen. I propose that we have a wrestling match between your wooden Buddha and my golden Buddha. If your Buddha loses, you must promise to work for me until you die. If my Buddha loses, however, I shall give you everything I own. I shall give you my house and everything in it, and you shall become master here. Do you agree?"

As the servant sat silently, pondering this strange offer, his master prodded him on. "Are you afraid your wooden Buddha will lose?" he asked. "Come, come, tell me what you think of this plan."

The servant thought of how he worshiped his Buddha, offering food and prayers three times a day. "But after all," he thought to himself, "he is only a piece of wood from the forest. How can he ever defeat a real, golden

Buddha in a wrestling match?" The servant didn't know what to do, for he was afraid to refuse his master's request, and yet he did not want to work there for the rest of his days.

Before he could say anything, however, the master called his other servants. "Listen!" he said gleefully. "I am going to let all of you see a wrestling match this afternoon." A happy murmur ran through the group of servants.

"What's more," the master went on, "it will be a very special match, for it will be between two Buddhas." And then, he went on to explain what would happen if the golden Buddha should lose, and what would happen if the wooden Buddha lost.

"Ahhhh," said the servants, whispering to one another. "This will be an interesting match indeed."

"You must all stay to watch," the master went on, "for you must help decide which of the Buddhas has won the match."

Then he turned to the servant saying, "Well, come, come. What are you waiting for? Bring forth your wonderful stick-of-wood Buddha."

And so the servant went trembling to his room and bowed before his wooden Buddha.

"Kibutsu-sama, Kibutsu-sama, a terrible thing has happened," he said, almost in tears. And he told the Buddha about the wrestling match his master proposed. "I do not want you to lose the match and be mocked in front of all those servants, and I do not want to work for this man till I die," said the servant. "The only thing left for me to do is to run away and take you with me."

But suddenly, the wooden Buddha spoke. "Wait a minute," he said. "Stop worrying. I will wrestle with the golden Buddha, and I will defeat him in this match! Come, let us go."

The servant looked up in surprise, for he had not expected to hear his Buddha answer. "Will you, good Buddha?" he asked. "Will you really defeat the golden Buddha?"

But before he could say more, he heard his master calling to him to hurry. He bowed once more in front of the Buddha. "I beg of you to do your best," he said, and picking up the wooden Buddha, he carried it outside.

In a patch of sand in the garden, the master had drawn a circle for the wrestling arena, and all around it stood the servants of the household who had come to watch. The two men set their Buddhas inside the circle and then stepped back. The servant held his breath. The master moved closer, and bending over his golden Buddha, he whispered, "You must win! You cannot lose!"

The servants all crowded around anxiously. Suddenly, the two Buddhas began to rock back and forth, coming closer and closer to each other until soon they were face to face. Then, they began to push and shove at each other, while the people watched in amazement.

At first, everyone watched silently, but soon, one of the servants began to shout, "Come on, golden one, you must win for our master! Knock him down!" Then another began to encourage the wooden Buddha. "Come on, you can win!" he called. "Knock down the golden one!"

Soon everyone in the garden was shouting and jumping up and down and stumbling over each other in excitement.

The great wrestling match went on for two hours, and for a while, it looked as though neither of them would win. But suddenly, the golden Buddha seemed to grow weary. He rocked this way and that, and tumbled wildly about the ring.

The master saw his Buddha weakening, and he shouted in a great loud voice over its head, "You can't lose! You can't lose to that stick of wood!" His face grew as red as a strawberry, and great beads of perspiration trickled down his forehead. But the more the master shouted, the weaker the golden Buddha seemed to become. Finally, with a loud metallic groan, the golden Buddha fell to the sand.

"Get up!" shouted the master. "Get up!" But the golden Buddha did not move.

The Wrestling Match of the Two Buddhas

Then, as everyone watched in silence, the wooden Buddha began to move, and headed straight for the master's house. There, he climbed into the family altar and took his place on the stand that once belonged to the golden Buddha. Then, he looked down at the people below as if to say, "This is my home now. I shall not be moved!"

The people of the household bowed down before the wooden Buddha saying, *"Namu ami dabutsu . . . namu ami dabutsu,* may Buddha be praised," and they worshiped before their new Buddha.

Now the servant who was once so poor became the new master of the house, and owned everything that once belonged to the man he had served.

The master was so disappointed, he didn't know what to do. But he had made a bold promise, and besides, he was the one who had proposed the match in the first place. There was nothing he could do but pack his things and leave the house. He put a few pieces of clothing in a *furoshiki,* picked up his golden Buddha, and walked sadly from the house. He looked back again and again, but no one even came out to bid him good-bye. No one came to wish him well.

"What a foolish man I was," he thought time and again, but there was nothing he could do about it now.

He wandered here and there, looking for a place to

work, but he did not know how to sweep or cook or clean, for servants had always done his work for him. People looked at his smooth, clean palms and said, "Ah, you have not worked before. We do not want to use you." And so he roamed from town to town carrying his golden Buddha.

"What a miserable life I have come to," he thought sadly, and one day he sat in the middle of an empty meadow and talked to his Buddha, for he had no one else to talk to.

"If only you hadn't lost that wrestling match!" he said forlornly. "What ever made you lose to a stick of wood like that?"

He looked accusingly at the golden Buddha, and was surprised to hear him answer.

"Don't blame me, my friend," the golden Buddha answered. "Even though that Buddha was only a piece of wood, the servant offered him food three times a day, and worshiped him with real devotion. How many times did you ever open the altar where I sat? You gave me food once or twice a year, and your prayers were hasty mutterings which you did not believe. You had no faith at all in me. Do you see now why I could not win the match?"

The master hung his head in shame.

"I was a foolish and selfish man," he said sadly. "If

only I had had the simple faith of my servant. If I had not been so greedy, I would never have proposed such a match, and neither you nor I would be in the sorry state we are today."

The man sat silently, thinking of all the things he should have done, and of all the mistakes he had made. But it was too late. Now he was penniless and without work. There was nothing at all in the wide world that he could call his own except the little golden Buddha he held clutched in his hand.

The Magic Mortar

Long, long ago, in a small village nestled beside the sea of Japan, there lived two brothers. The older brother was very wealthy and owned many things, but the younger brother was poor and had nothing.

One day, toward the end of December, when the people of the land were preparing to welcome the New Year, the younger brother went to his brother's home to borrow some rice.

"We have no rice for New Year's breakfast," he said. "Will you lend me just a little? I shall return it as soon as I can."

But the older brother was greedy, and he did not want to lend even a small amount of rice. "I haven't any to spare," he said, and he turned his brother away.

The young brother was sad and disappointed. He

walked slowly down the narrow dirt road that led back to his house. What would he say to his wife, coming home empty-handed? What would they eat on New Year's Day? He looked out at the cold blue sea, beating against the shore. He looked up at the murky skies full of the promise of snow, but he found no comfort anywhere. Scuffling along silently, he felt the wind sweep down from the mountains beyond, and thought of his empty charcoal bucket. It would be cold without coals in his *hibachi*.

As he walked along, he saw an old man with a long white beard working in the fields beside the road. He leaned against his hoe and called out, "Say there, young man! Why are you walking with your head down, looking so sad?"

"You would be sad too," the young man answered. "I am cold and hungry and my own brother will not even lend me rice for the New Year. The world is a sad and selfish place!"

"Come, now," the old man answered. "*All* the world is not so bad."

Then he handed the young man a small cake. "Here," he said. "Take this wheat cake and go to the shrine in the woods beyond. Behind the shrine you will see a big hole, and nearby will be many dwarfs. They will ask you for your wheat cake, but don't give it to them on any account, unless they agree to give you their stone mortar in exchange."

The young man thanked the farmer, and carrying the wheat cake carefully, he set off for the shrine in the woods. Just as the old man had said, behind the shrine was a big hole, and nearby were many dwarfs climbing in and out, tumbling and stumbling over each other. They were trying to lift a big log into their hole, and shouted and pushed as they got in each other's way. The young man bent down and picked up the log.

"Here, let me help you," he said, and lifting the log with one hand, he pushed it into the hole for them.

All at once, he heard a cry like the whine of a tiny mosquito. "Help! Murderer!" He looked down in alarm, and saw a tiny dwarf caught under his wooden clogs. He quickly picked him up, and as he did so, the tiny dwarf saw the wheat cake.

"What delicious thing is this?" he asked, sniffing hungrily. "It smells like all the good things I've ever eaten all rolled into one!"

"Why, this is just a wheat cake given to me by an old farmer," answered the young man.

"Please," begged the tiny dwarf. "Let me have that wheat cake. It will make a lovely dinner."

But the young man remembered what the farmer had said. "No, no," he said, shaking his head. "I can never let you have this wheat cake. It is very precious to me."

Soon, the other dwarfs clustered around. "Give us your wheat cake," they begged. But still the young man shook his head.

Then the dwarfs brought out big bags of gold. "Here," they said. "We will give you all this gold if you will just let us have that wheat cake."

But again, the young man shook his head. "No, no," he said, "I'll not trade this wheat cake for all the gold in the world."

"Not for all the gold in the world? Why, this must be a very special and most wonderful wheat cake," the dwarfs said. "What do you want for it, if you will not take gold?"

"Well, let me see," the young man said, looking around. Then, he saw the stone mortar the old man had told him about. "I will give you my wheat cake if you will give me that stone mortar," he said.

The dwarfs put their heads together and talked noisily. At last, they agreed. "All right," they said. "Although it is a very special mortar, we will let you have it in exchange for your wheat cake."

Then the tiny dwarf spoke up. "This is a magic mortar, you know. It will give you anything you ask for if you turn it to the right. Then, when you've had enough, turn it to the left and it will stop."

The Magic Mortar

The young man thanked the dwarfs for the mortar and gave them his wheat cake. Before he could even turn around, they had gathered about the cake and were making a great commotion that sounded like a thousand mosquitoes buzzing in the air. The young man slipped away quietly and set off for home. This time, he walked with his head up, whistling a gay tune. He looked up at the tall cedar trees that reached out to the sun, and his own glad heart soared into the sky with them.

When he got home, his wife was waiting anxiously for him in the cold house. "What were you doing for so long?" she asked. "I have been waiting and waiting for you to bring home the rice!"

"But I have brought home something even better than a bag of rice," the young man said, and he told his wife about the old man with the white beard, and about the mortar the dwarfs had given him.

"Hurry then," the wife said. "Let's see if the mortar really works."

So they spread a clean mat on the *tatami* and placed the mortar in the center.

"Now," the young man said. "What would you like first?"

The wife thought for only a moment. "Oh, I would like some rice," she said, "so I can make rice cakes for New Year's Day."

The young man slowly turned the mortar to the right.
"Mortar, mortar, make some rice!" he called out, and slowly, slowly, the mortar began to fill with clean white rice. It was soon so full, it overflowed, and rice spilled out everywhere. The young man let the mortar make enough rice to last the whole new year, and then, turning it to the left, he told it to stop.

Next, he decided he would like some wine.

"Mortar, mortar, make some wine!" he commanded, and as he turned it, the mortar filled with clear white wine.

One after the other, he produced all kinds of wonderful things from the mortar, until he had enough to have a great feast on New Year's Day.

"What an amazing thing the dwarfs gave me," the young man thought happily. And the next morning, he decided to ask for a bigger house, for he now had so many wonderful things his little house could not hold them all.

"Mortar, mortar, please give us a bigger house," he said.

Suddenly, there was a blinding flash. The young man and his wife blinked their eyes, and when they opened them again, they found themselves sitting inside a beautiful big mansion. Outside, there was a lovely garden with a wooden bridge that curved over a glistening pond. There was even a stable with many fine horses that stood swishing their tails, waiting for someone to ride on them.

The young man and his wife looked wonderingly at their new home, and decided they would invite all their friends to visit this beautiful estate.

"Make rice! Make wine! Make fish and chicken and lotus root!" they said to the mortar, and then they invited their friends and neighbors to a big celebration. Everyone came dressed in their best kimonos, and looked with curious eyes at the house and all the good things to eat.

"How strange it is," they said to one another. "How can it be, when only yesterday they didn't even have rice for the New Year?" But even as they wondered, they were glad for the young brother, for he had always been a good and kind man.

Because he was also forgiving and generous, he had even invited his older brother who had been so unkind to him the day before.

The older brother came and looked about in amazement. "This is very strange indeed," he said to himself, and over and over he asked the younger brother how he had suddenly become so wealthy.

"Tell me how it happened," he asked.

But the younger brother merely smiled and said, "I was very lucky, that's all."

When the guests were about to leave, the young brother thought he would like to give each of them some sweet cakes to take home. He opened the cupboard, took out the magic mortar and told it to make some cakes. Just as he was doing this, the older brother passed by and saw what he was doing.

"So!" he said to himself. "That is how my poor brother suddenly got so much money and food!" And he went off into the garden to think of a way in which he could get his brother's mortar.

When all the guests had gone, the older brother asked if he might spend the night there. "The night is cold, and I do not like to walk home in the darkness. Let me stay with you tonight," he asked.

And so the younger brother spread an extra quilt on the floor, and the older brother lay down, pretending to go to sleep. He waited until the others were sound asleep, and then he tiptoed to the cupboard, stole the magic mortar, and slipped out into the dark night. He ran with the mortar under his arm until he came to the edge of the sea. There he found a little boat on the beach.

"Just what I need to help me get away," he said, and he jumped into the boat. Then he decided he would row out to one of the little islands in the sea. There he would use the mortar and become the wealthiest man of the land.

"Ah, I shall live a good life," he thought happily.

But as he rowed on, his arms began to ache and grow

weary. He decided to stop and have something to eat, but all he could find in the bundle he brought along were a few unsalted rice cakes. He looked about, wishing he had brought along some salt, when suddenly he remembered the stone mortar he had stolen.

"Now is the time to test it," he thought, and turning it to the right, as he had seen his brother do, he said, "Mortar, mortar, make some salt!"

Slowly, the mortar began to fill with salt, and soon it overflowed into the boat.

"That's enough! Stop!" cried the older brother, but he didn't know how to make the mortar stop. Soon, the whole boat was filled with salt, and as it grew heavier it sank deeper and deeper into the water.

"Help! The boat will sink!" the older brother shouted, but there was no one out in the middle of the sea to hear him. The waves lapped higher and higher and soon swallowed the little boat, taking the mortar and the brother down to the very bottom of the sea.

On top of the water, only a mass of white bubbles gleamed in the moonlight, but down at the bottom of the sea, the mortar continued to make salt. Because no one ever went down to turn it to the left and tell it to stop, salt still flows from the mortar. And that is why, they say, the sea is salty even today.

The Tubmaker
Who Flew to the Sky

Long, long ago, there lived in Japan a man who earned his living by making tubs and barrels. He made great wide tubs for baths, he made tall high barrels for wine, and he made short squat tubs for soy sauce. He worked hard from morning till night, and the sound of hammering and pounding always filled the air around his shop.

One day, a wine merchant hurried into his shop and called out to him, "Make me three large barrels by tomorrow morning." And then, before the tubmaker could tell him how busy he was, he ran out of the shop and disappeared down the street.

The tubmaker shook his head and hurried outside behind his shop. There, in his small yard, he began to fit the barrel staves together, hammering and pounding until his arms ached. When, at last, he was fitting the hoops around the last barrel, a strange thing happened. The hoop suddenly snapped with a WHANNNNNG, and caught the tubmaker by the sleeves. Before he knew what was happening, he was swept into the air with a swoosh, and was sailing up into the sky.

"Whhhat's happening? Where am I?" the tubmaker muttered to himself. He was flying up, up, and up, higher and higher still, until soon he was soaring into the clouds.

Suddenly, he stopped, and when he looked around, he discovered he had landed right in the middle of a big gray cloud. When he finally caught his breath and looked up, he saw the great god of thunder standing in front of him.

"Well, well," the thunder god roared. "What have we here?" He bent down to look at the tubmaker who sat with his legs crossed on the gray softness of the cloud. The tubmaker felt the cold icy breath of the thunder god as he bent down to inspect him, and he was filled with a great and terrible fear.

"I . . . I . . . I . . ." he began, but his teeth chattered so, he could not talk.

"Well, well! Out with it," said the thunder god. "What are you trying to tell me?"

And so the tubmaker took a deep breath and began again. "I . . . I . . . I've come from Japan . . . down

44

below. . . . I was fitting the hoop on a wine barrel, when suddenly, before I knew what was happening, I was sailing up into the sky."

The tubmaker shook his head. He still couldn't believe what had happened. "It was very strange," he said wonderingly. "Very strange indeed. A hoop has never snapped like that before."

The tubmaker looked sad and forlorn, but the thunder god laughed with a great thunderous roar. "HA, HA, HA! You must have been a funny sight," he said. "I've seen birds flying this high, but I've never seen a human being up here before."

Then the god suddenly seemed to remember what he was doing. "You've come just in time," he said. "I've been meaning to send some rain down below for a long time, but my assistant who carries my water sacks has disappeared. I was just looking for someone to help me."

The tubmaker looked around, but no assistant rainmaker was in sight. He looked up and saw that the thunder god was looking right at him. "Do you mean you'd like me to help you?" he asked timidly.

"You're a trifle small," the thunder god said, "but I think you'll do."

Then he handed the tubmaker an enormous sack filled with water, and standing very straight and tall, he began to beat on his eight great drums.

"WHANNG . . . CRASH . . . BANG . . . BOOM!" The drums roared and rumbled and sounded like a thousand lions about to eat him up. The tubmaker held his hands over his ears and closed his eyes tight. But soon, he heard the thunder god calling to him.

"Now, let the rain fall!" he roared.

So, the tubmaker opened his eyes, raised the sack, and began to pour water on the earth below. Soon, thunder roared, lightning flashed, and great torrents of water went rushing down from the great gray clouds.

"Keep pouring! Keep pouring!" shouted the thunder god, and he handed the tubmaker one sack of water after the other.

As the tubmaker looked down, he could see everything that was going on below. People were rushing and scurrying and running for cover. "What a terrible storm!" they shouted, as they ran this way and that.

Watching from the sky, the tubmaker laughed as he saw the commotion he had caused. Here was a woman dropping her laundry as she hurried to take it off the long bamboo poles. Over there was a farmer running home from the fields, holding a straw cape over his head. He slipped and stumbled as he ran on the wet road, and was covered with mud from head to toe.

"My, those little people look funny," thought the tubmaker. And he was having such a good time, he wished he could always live high above the earth and watch the tiny people below. He was so busy looking down, he scarcely paid any attention to what he was doing. He hopped merrily from cloud to cloud, whistling and singing, and letting the water pour out from the big sacks of rain.

"Have some rain, little people," he sang. "Have some rain!"

Suddenly, just as he was hopping from one cloud to the next, his foot slipped. Still clutching one of the big sacks of rain, the tubmaker felt himself falling off the cloud.

"Help!" he shouted to the thunder god, but by the time the god turned around, it was too late. His assistant had already zoomed down through the gray skies and fallen to earth.

"I hope I land in a nice soft rice paddy," he thought. But when he finally stopped and opened his eyes, he found he had landed right on top of a very tall tree growing in the yard of the village temple. The tubmaker peered down cautiously. The ground was covered with puddles that his rain had made. He wanted to call for help, but the yard was quiet and empty, and not a single priest was in sight. The tubmaker sat in the tree and waited for a long time. Soon, it grew cold, and he began to shiver as the wind began to blow.

"Help!" he shouted. "Help!" But he was so far up, no one could hear him. A few birds flew by and looked at him curiously, but they were no help to him at all.

"I wonder if I will have to stay here forever," thought the tubmaker gloomily. "I would give anything to be back down on the ground again."

As he sat wondering what to do, he saw a priest walking slowly through the yard. "Help!" he shouted in his loudest, strongest voice. The priest thought he heard someone calling, and he looked to the left and he looked to the right. Still, he couldn't see a soul.

"Up here!" shouted the tubmaker. "I'm up here!"

"The voice seems to be coming from the tree top," said the priest. He was old and he could not see very well. He squinted through his glasses and at last saw the tubmaker waving frantically from the highest limb of the ginkgo tree.

"Ah . . . ah . . ." said the old priest. "What are you doing up there? Come down at once! It's dangerous to be up so high."

"I know it's dangerous," shouted the tubmaker. "I want to come down, but I can't. Help me!"

The old priest scratched his head. "Wait!" he called. "I'll go for help."

Soon all the priests of the temple came out and looked

up at the tubmaker perched like a big black crow on the highest limb of their ginkgo tree.

"Hmmmm, how very strange," they said. "I wonder how he ever got up there."

The tubmaker watched them as they clustered in a little circle and wondered how to get him down. "If we only had a ladder," they said. "But there is no ladder that will reach quite that high."

At last the priests seemed to have thought of something, and they ran back into the temple.

"Come back! Don't leave me up here!" the tubmaker shouted.

Soon they were back with a big blanket which they stretched out beneath the tree. Holding on to its edges, they called to the tubmaker, "Jump! We'll catch you!"

Now the blanket looked terribly small and terribly far away, but the tubmaker decided he would either have to jump or stay in the tree for the rest of his life.

"All right," he called in a small weak voice. "I'll jump."

He took a deep breath, closed his eyes, and took a big leap. PLOP and PLUNK . . . He landed right in the middle of the blanket, bouncing like a rubber ball.

"How good it is to be back on earth!" the tubmaker said gratefully, and bowing low, he thanked each of the priests who had caught him in the blanket. Then he hurried home to his shop where the barrels and tubs still waited for him.

"My, it's good to be back," he thought happily. He looked up to see if he could see the great thunder god peering down at him from one of the clouds, but all he could see was the clear night sky covered with thousands of stars that seemed to be laughing at him.

The tubmaker wondered if it was all a dream, for there wasn't a single rain cloud in the whole night sky. He looked around his shop, and then he looked at the barrels he had been working on that morning. Yes, there was the broken hoop that had sent him into the sky. And, yes, the barrels were filled with the very rain he had poured down from the gray cloud.

The tubmaker smiled as he thought of his strange adventure. He picked up his hammer and repaired the broken hoop of his wine barrel so it would be ready for the wine merchant in the morning. But this time, he was very, very careful not to get his sleeve caught again.

It was great fun helping the thunder god, but it was even better being down on earth in his own little shop. And from that day on, the tubmaker was careful to keep both feet planted firmly on the ground.

Three Tests for the Prince

Once upon a time, there lived in Japan a powerful ruler named Susano. He lived high on a hill in a beautiful palace with his only child, a lovely princess. Because he was haughty and proud, he kept everyone away from the palace, so the young princess was often lonely and very sad.

One day, there was much noise at the front gate of the palace, and Susano commanded the princess to see who had come. She hurried to the gate and found a young man who looked as if he had come on a long journey. He was tired and dusty, but when the princess saw his face, she knew he was no ordinary traveler.

She returned to her father and said, "It is a young man who has come from afar. His face is good and kind, and his eyes are like the stars in heaven."

Susano thought for a moment and then laughed. "Ho, ho," he said. "This must be another prince who has come to ask for your hand."

When the princess heard this, she felt sorry for the young man, for there had been many others who had come before him. But all of them had been treated so unkindly by her father, they ran away and never came back.

"Oh me," she sighed. And her sigh was like a breeze filtering through a bamboo grove. It was so faint and had come from so deep inside her that Susano did not even hear it.

"Very well," he continued. "I shall test the courage of this young prince. Take him to the Room of the Snakes."

The princess shuddered. "The Room of the Snakes!" she said. "Why, you only send your enemies to that horrible room. He has come from far away, and you are so cruel." She trembled when she thought of the cold dark room where hundreds of snakes slithered out of the walls each night.

"We shall see how brave your young man is," Susano said, and he would not listen although the princess begged him to be kind.

So the princess went to greet the young man saying, "My father will receive you tomorrow." Then, leading him to the Room of the Snakes, she added, "He would like you to spend the night here."

The prince bowed low. "Ah, he is most kind," he said.

But the princess was filled with pity, and she said in a sudden whisper, "No, no, my father is not kind at all. He is cruel and selfish, and he has sent you to this terrible room to test your courage."

"I'm not afraid," the prince answered.

"But you don't understand," the princess went on. "Tonight this room will be filled with hissing snakes. They will come from every crack in the wall and the ceiling and even the floor. It will be horrible!"

Then she drew out a beautiful blue scarf and handed it to the prince. "Take this," she urged, "and when the snakes come, wave it over your head three times. They will not touch you and will disappear again into the walls."

The princess hurried away and closed the door behind her. "What a good and gentle princess," the prince thought, and he stretched out on the quilt and went to sleep. Shortly after midnight, he awoke with a start. The room seemed to be filled with terrible hissing noises, and the prince remembered what the princess had told him. He reached for the blue scarf and waved it three times over his head. The hissing stopped and the snakes disappeared. It was just as the princess had said. The prince went back to sleep and didn't waken until morning when the sun began to filter into his room.

When the prince appeared before Susano, the first thing he asked was, "How did you sleep last night, young man?"

"Very well, thank you," the prince answered quietly.

"Did nothing disturb you?" Susano asked.

"Nothing at all," answered the prince. "I was so tired, I slept very well."

"Hmmmm," said Susano, rubbing his chin. "And did you not hear any strange sounds?"

The prince shook his head. "I heard nothing," he said.

Susano could not understand what had happened. The second night, he was determined to test the courage of the prince once more.

"Put him in the Room of the Bees and Centipedes," he commanded.

And so the princess led the prince again to another terrible room.

"Tonight this room will be filled with stinging bees and crawling centipedes," the princess warned. "But don't be frightened," she added. "Wave my scarf over your head three times, and nothing will harm you."

"Thank you, kind princess," the prince said. "I do not feel frightened at all."

That night after the prince had gone to sleep, he was

awakened by the sound of thousands of buzzing bees. He quickly waved the magic scarf over his head, and the bees and centipedes all disappeared. Once again, the prince had a good night's sleep.

Early the next morning, Susano called the young prince before him. "How did you sleep last night?" he asked. "Even better than the night before," the prince answered.

"Did you hear nothing? Did you feel nothing?" Susano continued.

"I slept soundly," the prince said. "I felt nothing and I heard nothing."

"This is very strange," thought Susano to himself, and he wondered if there wasn't some way he could frighten the prince away.

Suddenly he had a plan. "Follow me," he said, and he led the prince out into the field behind the palace. Susano carried a great bow and a quiver full of arrows, and the prince thought he would probably be asked to have a shooting match with him.

"If Susano shoots his arrow one hundred feet, I shall shoot mine two hundred," the prince thought to himself, and he watched silently as Susano lifted the heavy bow and aimed high into the sky. With a great ZINNNNNNG, the arrow sped into the air and disappeared somewhere in the hills beyond the field.

The prince reached for the bow to take his turn, but Susano shook his head. "Your task, young prince, is to find that arrow wherever it may have fallen," he said.

"But the grass is deep and an arrow is small," the prince answered. "Surely you must know what an impossible task that would be."

But Susano only glared silently at the prince. "If you have come for my daughter's hand, you must pass this final test," he answered, and he left the prince standing sadly in the middle of the field.

There was nothing for the prince to do but to set off for the distant hill. He searched among the tall dry grass as he walked, but the farther he went, the taller the grass seemed to grow. As he walked along, looking down at the ground, he suddenly began to smell smoke. The prince looked up and saw that the dry grass of the hillside was ablaze with flames that shot wildly in all directions. The prince turned to go back, but leaping flames cut off his path. He looked around wondering which way to go, but smoke closed in all around him like a thick, heavy fog.

"Ah, the wicked Susano must have started this fire," the prince thought angrily. "Surely, he is the cruelest ruler that ever lived." And he stumbled through the smoke, wondering if he would die in the flames.

Suddenly, he heard a squeaking at his feet, and looking down, he saw a tiny field mouse. The mouse ran around his feet, pulling at his legs. "What is it, little fellow? Are you caught in the fire too?" the prince asked.

And to his surprise, the mouse answered back. "Come quickly, prince. It is dangerous here. Come with me to my home," and the mouse scampered through the grass to a small dark hole in the ground.

"You are very kind, little mouse," the prince said, "but as you can see, I am much too big for your little house."

"No, no," the mouse said, shaking his head. "It is much bigger inside than you think."

The prince put his foot into the hole and wriggled it around. Soon, the dirt fell away, and the hole was big enough for the prince to crawl right in. The mouse led him through a deep, dark tunnel far, far beneath the ground. It was cool and quiet down there, and they could hear the distant roar of the fire as it passed over their heads.

"Thank you, little mouse," the prince said gratefully. "You have surely saved my life today."

The mouse scurried away then, and came back with something in his mouth.

"Is this what you were looking for when I found you today?" he said. And the mouse handed the prince the arrow that Susano had shot into the air.

"Why, this is the very arrow I was looking for," the prince said happily. "How did you ever find it?"

The mouse simply flicked his whiskers and looked the other way. "I know a great many things," he said. "And I wanted to help you and the gentle princess. Go quickly now, for she will be looking for you."

So the prince thanked the mouse again, and hurried off through the charred woods, back to the palace at the top of the hill.

When he returned, he found the princess sadly making preparations for a funeral for him.

"I thought surely you had died in those terrible flames," she said. "How glad I am to see that you are safe and well!"

"I am glad too, dear princess," the prince said, and then he turned to Susano and handed him the arrow. "Here, sir, is the arrow you shot into the air this morning."

"But that was an impossible task," Susano said wonderingly. "How did you ever find it?"

"I was very lucky," the prince answered, but he did not tell Susano about the little field mouse who had helped him.

Susano was baffled and annoyed to think the prince had passed such a difficult test. He went off to his room to sulk and to think of still another way to get rid of the

prince. He lay down and closed his eyes, and soon he
was sound asleep.

When the prince saw that Susano was asleep, he crept
into his room without making a sound. Then he parted
the hair on Susano's head and tied half to a chair, and
the other half to the leg of a table.

"There," he said. "That should keep you still for a
while."

Then he tiptoed out of the room and rolled a big
boulder in front of the door so Susano could not get out.

Quickly, he ran in search of the princess and said, "I
have tied up your wicked father. Come quickly, and we
shall both escape from him forever."

The princess gathered her three greatest treasures—a
sword, a quiver of arrows, and the jewels her mother had
left her. Then she and the prince hurried to get out of
the palace before Susano awoke. Just as they reached the
gate, however, the arrows and the sword clattered to the
ground. They made a terrible crash that rang through the
empty halls of the palace.

"What was that?" shouted Susano, and he tried to get
up, but he could not move his head.

"Who has done this terrible thing to me?" he cried
angrily, and he untied his hair and ran to the door. But
the door would not open for the boulder was in front of
it. By the time he pushed the boulder out of the way, the

prince and princess were safely on the road that led into the woods.

Susano ran to the palace gate and looked down at the winding road.

"Stop!" he shouted to the two tiny figures that he saw riding away toward the hills. "Come back! Come back!" he called.

But the wind carried his voice back to him in a lonely echo, and the prince and princess did not even turn to look back.

Susano shook his head sadly and went into the palace all alone.

Because he had been so cruel, he had lost his only beautiful daughter. Now there was nothing in the world left for him except his empty palace and his own selfish wickedness.

The prince and the princess escaped to a land far away from Susano's palace, and together lived many long and happy years.

The Deer of Five Colors

Once long ago, there lived a deer more beautiful than any in the whole world, for his coat was five-colored, and his antlers were whiter than new-fallen snow. He lived alone deep in a forest of pine where no man ever walked, and his only friend was a jet-black crow. Each day the crow would fly over the deer's head, and together they would roam the quiet hills. Sometimes they basked in the warmth of the sun, listening to the water of the river as it rushed by over pebbles and stones. Sometimes, they would climb high to the top of a mountain and look down at the neat green fields that spread out around the villages below. They lived happily and peacefully, and were bothered by no living man.

One day, however, a farmer chanced to walk through the forest on his way back from a distant village. The sun had already slipped down over the hills and the forest was filled with shadows. The farmer hurried as he walked along the river bank, and in his haste, his foot slipped in the mud. Before he knew what was happening, he had tumbled into the river and was carried downstream by the swift current. The farmer tried to swim, but the water was cold, for it came from the snow that melted on the mountains above.

"Help!" the farmer shouted weakly, but there was no one in the lonely forest to hear him.

"Help! Please save me!" he called again. "I'm drowning! I'm drowning!"

And this time, the beautiful five-colored deer heard his pitiful cries. He ran swiftly through the forest and came to the edge of the river. There, he saw the man floundering in the water and calling for help. The deer plunged into the icy water, caught the man by his coat, and pulled him safely to shore.

The man was so grateful, he clasped his hands together and bowed low before the deer. "You have saved my life," he said. "What can I ever do to repay you? I shall be glad to do anything you say."

But the deer shook his head. "There is no need for you to do anything for me," he said. "The only thing I ask is that you promise not to tell anyone you saw me in this forest."

The farmer nodded solemnly. "I shall never tell," he promised. "But why do you make such a strange request?"

Then the deer answered. "Look at me. My coat is of five colors and my antlers are white. There is no deer anywhere on earth that looks like me. I know that men are greedy and cruel, and there are many who would kill me to sell my hide for gold. That is why I have hidden deep in this forest all these years, far away from the villages of men. You must promise never to tell anyone you saw me, for if you tell, surely someone will come to hunt me, and I shall be captured and killed."

"I promise," the farmer said over and over again. "I shall never tell anyone that you live in this forest."

And then, bowing and waving to the beautiful deer, the farmer hurried home to his village. There he worked hard each day, planting his rice and wheat and harvesting his crops. Sometimes he would look up toward the forest in the hills and think about the five-colored deer that had saved his life. But he remembered his promise, and never told a living soul about this strange and beautiful creature that feared the arrows of man.

One day, however, the ruler of the land sent a message to all the villages and towns near and far. A messenger came bearing a notice that said the great lord had had a strange dream. He had dreamed of a beautiful five-colored deer with antlers as white as snow. "Surely," he had said, "if I have dreamed of such an animal, it must exist somewhere in this land of mine. I shall give a plot of land as well as gold and silver and precious jewels to any man who can lead me to this five-colored deer."

Now when the farmer heard this, he thought of the house he could build and the servants he could hire if he became a wealthy man.

"I wouldn't have to get up each morning before the sun and work till my back is about to break. I could eat whatever I pleased and live like the great lord himself," he thought. And as he mused about these things, he forgot the promise he had once made to the beautiful five-colored deer. He left his plow in the field, and his oxen standing in the sun, and hurried to the palace of the great lord.

"I can lead the lord to the five-colored deer he saw in his dreams," he said eagerly.

So the very next day, the farmer was commanded to lead the lord and his party to the forest where the deer lived. He rode in front, and behind him followed the lord and his huntsmen carrying great bows and arrows. The farmer led the men along the banks of the very river in which he once had almost drowned, and up the wooded path into the hills.

As the sound of the horses' hoofs thudded along the

dirt road, the black crow of the forest heard, and hurried to the side of the five-colored deer.

"Run! Run!" he called to the deer. "The lord and his men are coming to kill you. Hide quickly!"

But the deer was asleep in the sun, and would not wake up.

"Quickly! Wake up! The lord and his hunters have come with bows and arrows!" the crow shrieked.

At last the deer opened his eyes, but it was too late. He could already hear the horses and the voices of the lord and his men.

"Why do you not hide, my friend," the crow said sadly, but the deer did not even seem to be afraid.

"I will talk to this lord. I will not run," said the deer, "for if they see me running, they will only shoot me."

And so the deer stood in an opening and waited for the lord to come. As soon as the hunters saw the deer standing in the sunlight, his white antlers glistening in the sun, they raised their bows and arrows and took aim.

Just as they were about to shoot, the lord shouted, "Stop! Don't kill him! If he is bold enough to come into the open to meet the men who hunt him, he must surely have something to say." The deer came before the lord and spoke in a low voice.

"I am the five-colored deer you seek," he said. "For many years now, I have hidden in this forest, for I knew that if I were discovered, men would kill me to sell my hide. How did you know where to find me?"

Then the lord turned to the farmer and pointed to him. "He is the man who led us to your forest," he said. "It was he who told us that the five-colored deer I saw in my dream really lived in my land."

The deer turned to the farmer. "Have you forgotten so soon?" he asked. "Do you not remember the day when I saved your life and you asked what you could do to repay me? I said then that I wanted nothing. All I asked was your promise that you would never tell anyone where I lived, for if you did, I would surely be captured and killed."

The farmer hung his head in shame, and could not look at the deer.

"I risked my own life that day in the icy waters of the river to save your life," the deer went on. "And you have repaid my kindness today by leading these men to capture and kill me."

The lord turned to the farmer in surprise. "Is this true?" he asked. "Did this deer once save your life?"

The farmer nodded. "It is true," he said in a low voice. "And today I betrayed him because of my greed. When I thought of the gold and silver I would receive, I forgot the promise I once made to him."

"Then you are a worthless man who does not deserve

to be free," the lord said angrily, and he commanded that the farmer be thrown in jail to live in the darkness of a cell the rest of his days.

Then he turned to the deer saying, "You risked your own life to save the life of this man. Surely you are far nobler and kinder than this miserable creature who loves gold more than another's life. You shall not be captured today or ever after. Go back to your forest and live in peace."

The lord then spoke to his men, saying, "Lower your bows and arrows. There shall be no deer hunted in my land, for I have learned today that the deer is an animal nobler than man."

Then the kind-hearted lord returned to his palace with his men. And from that day on, he and the people of his land prospered and lived in peace.

The beautiful five-colored deer returned to the forest he loved, and there, no longer fearing the huntsmen, he and his friend, the black crow, lived happily in the quiet peace of the hills.

The Golden Axe

Long, long ago, there were two woodcutters who lived next door to each other. One was a good and kind man, but he was very, very poor. And because he was old, he had to get up each morning while the stars were still out in order to chop enough wood to sell in the village. With the money he earned from selling wood, he was able to buy just enough food for his wife and himself. Now his neighbor was a young man who was greedy and selfish. He had much more money, but he never helped the poor woodcutter next door. Instead, he laughed at him for having to work so hard.

"Poor old fellow," he would say to the woodcutter. "You can't make a living even with all the hard work you do. Why don't you get up at four o'clock instead of five, then maybe you could earn more money!"

And he taunted the old woodcutter as he came home at dusk, carrying a small bag of rice and dried fish—the only food he could afford to buy.

One day, the kind woodcutter went out to chop wood in the mountains as usual. He got up especially early, for it was a fine morning.

"I think I'll be able to chop much wood today," he said to his wife, and he trudged up the mountain path.

He went to his favorite spot beside a quiet pool and took out his axe. He liked to work there, for when he grew tired, he could sit down and watch the water ripple gently in the breeze. He liked to look up and see the clouds marching in the blueness of the sky. Then he would look down, and there they were again reflected in his own little pool, with the tall cedars stretching all around it. The old man thought there was no place in the world quite so peaceful and beautiful.

"Ah, what a lovely morning it is!" he said, and singing in a loud voice, the old man began to chop down a tree. He swung his axe high into the air and sang out, "*Yoisho . . . yoisho! Dokkoi-sho!*"

The sound of the axe rang through the forest and echoed from tree to tree. The old man worked hard and long. Suddenly, as he swung upward, the blade of the axe flew off the handle and went flying into the air. Before the old man realized what had happened, he heard a splash, and knew it had fallen into the pool. The old woodcutter hurried to the pool and looked in, but all he could see were big circles growing wider and wider on the surface of the water. He stood silently for a few moments, wondering what to do.

"What shall I do? What shall I do?" he murmured sadly. "The pool is deep and I am too old to dive in and look for the blade."

Looking into the water, he thought of the money it would cost to buy a new axe. "I cannot afford to buy a new axe now," he thought. "But without an axe I can chop no more wood." He sat forlornly at the edge of the pool and prayed to the goddess of the water.

"Please, dear goddess, help me to find my axe," the old man prayed. "Without my axe I cannot work, and if I do not work my wife and I will not be able to eat."

As the old man sat gazing into the depths of the pool, there suddenly arose a cloud of mist. Milky waves of fog seemed to be floating up from the bottom of the pool. The old man rubbed his eyes, for suddenly, in the midst of the whiteness that enclosed the pool, he saw the goddess of the water herself. She stood glimmering in a golden robe, and in her hand she held something that shone brighter than the sun itself. The old woodcutter fell to his knees and bowed his head.

"Is this what you were looking for?" the goddess

asked. And she held out a golden axe toward the old man.

The old man blinked hard. "But this is not my axe," he said. "This one is made of gold, and mine was only a poor one made of steel. There must be some mistake."

The goddess smiled and took back the golden axe. "Wait a moment, old man," she said, and slowly, slowly, she descended again into the depths of the pool. When she came up again, she carried in her hand the old axe blade of the woodcutter.

"Is this one yours then?" she asked.

The old man's heart sang with happiness. "Yes, yes!" he answered. "How can I ever thank you. Now I shall be able to cut down more trees and my wife and I need not go hungry."

The old man bowed low, touching his forehead to the ground.

"You are a good and honest man," the goddess said. "And I know how hard you work each day, for I hear the sound of your axe from early morning till late in the evening. Not many people would have been as honest as you were today," she went on. "And to reward your honesty, I shall give you this golden axe."

The old man was so surprised he could not speak. He gazed at the golden axe that sparkled in his hand. When he looked up to thank the goddess, she had already disappeared into the pool. The mist was gone, and the water glistened once more in the sunlight. The old man stood for a long while, looking down into the pool. He wondered if the goddess lived in a beautiful golden palace down at the very bottom. He looked hard, but all he could see were the branches of trees reflected on the surface of the pool. There wasn't even a ripple to stir the stillness.

"It must have been a dream," the old man thought to himself. But he looked down, and there was the golden axe. Beside it lay his steel blade, still damp and wet.

"It wasn't a dream after all!" the old man said happily. "It really did happen!"

And without cutting any more trees that day, he hurried down the mountainside to tell his wife what had happened.

"Look!" he shouted as he ran home. And quickly, he told his wife about the goddess of the water and the golden axe.

Soon, the people of the village heard about the good fortune that had befallen the old woodcutter and came to celebrate with him.

"We are happy for you. You surely deserved it, for you have always been good and kind," they all said to him, and they brought gifts of rice and fish and wine.

And it was a strange thing, but from that day on, the

old woodcutter never had to worry about having enough money. There always seemed to be plenty of coins in his bag and plenty of rice in the bin. The old woodcutter and his wife knew that somehow the golden axe had changed the pattern of their life. They kept it carefully in a wooden box, and bowed before it each day, thanking the goddess of the water for having brought them such good fortune.

Now when the woodcutter next door saw what had happened to his neighbor, he wanted more than anything in the world to have a golden axe just like the old man's.

"Surely, if that old woodcutter can get a golden axe from the goddess of the water, I should be able to get one too," he thought, and he went to ask his neighbor just how he got it.

"Tell me exactly what happened," he said over and over again, until at last he knew all the details of that sunny morning when the axe blade flew off the handle. Then, he hurried off into the mountains and looked for the spot where the old man liked to work. As soon as he found the pool, he picked a tree very close to the water's edge and began to chop. *"Yoisho! Yoisho!"* he cried, swinging the axe with all his might. He struck hard and he swung high, but the blade of his axe was firm and would not loosen.

He chopped and he chopped, but still the blade would not come off. Suddenly, the woodcutter became angry.

"Stupid axe!" he shouted, and picking up a sharp stone, he hammered at the blade until it broke off from the handle.

"Now, let's see what happens," he said, and he flung the blade into the pool. He watched the circles widen and spread out over the water, and when he thought the goddess had seen the blade, he cried out in a loud voice.

"Dear goddess of the water," he said. "Please help me to find my axe, for without it I cannot work and I shall starve to death."

Soon, misty vapors rose from the pool, and again, the goddess appeared in her golden robe, carrying a golden axe in her hand.

"Is this the axe you were looking for?" she asked.

"Ah, you are most kind," the woodcutter said, and he reached out eagerly to take the golden axe. "This is indeed my own axe. I cannot thank you enough for finding it for me."

But as the woodcutter bowed, the goddess took the axe away from him.

"You lie, woodcutter! You lie!" she said. "This is not your own axe blade." Her voice was full of anger and she looked sternly at the woodcutter. "You are a dishonest and greedy man, and for that you will suffer the rest of your days."

Without another word, she disappeared into the water, leaving the greedy woodcutter sitting all alone in the woods.

"Come back!" he called after her. "I will take my own steel blade, if you will just come back!"

The woodcutter waited, but only the sound of his own cries filled the forest, and the goddess did not return. He looked down sadly at the broken handle of his axe. He did not have the golden axe, and besides that, he had lost his own best steel axe.

"How foolish I have been," he thought, but it was too late. He walked home slowly, his head bent low.

When he got home, his wife was greatly excited. "Where is it? Let me see the golden axe!" she cried. But the woodcutter only lifted his two empty hands and shrugged his shoulders.

"But didn't you do as the woodcutter next door?" the wife shrieked at him. "Look at the food I've bought. I've told everyone to come tonight to see our golden axe. What will we do? What will we do?"

But there was nothing in the world the woodcutter could do. He couldn't even go out to chop more wood, for his axe lay at the bottom of the mountain pool.

"How will we pay for all this food?" his wife wailed. But the woodcutter did not answer her. "We were foolish to be so greedy," he said sadly. And from that day on, he never tried again to imitate his good neighbor.

The Mountain Witch and the Peddler

There once lived a peddler in a small village beside the Japan Sea. One day, when he could no longer sell his salted mackerel in his own village, he decided he would take them to the village beyond the mountains.

He strapped two barrels of salt mackerel on his horse and set off. The path was narrow and steep and the journey took much longer than he thought it would.

"I should have started out earlier," he thought as he trudged along the lonely path.

As he wound his way up and up into the mountains, he looked around and saw the tall cedar and pine trees stretching silently all about him. Nothing seemed to stir, not even the birds or the animals of the forest. Gradually, the air began to grow cold and the peddler saw the sun slipping behind the highest peak in the west. He felt a cold loneliness pass through his heart, and he wished he had never left his nice warm home. But it was too late now to turn back, and so he trudged on, silently and alone.

Suddenly, he heard footsteps behind him. "Ah, it will be good to have someone to talk to," he thought, and he looked back to see who was traveling the lonely road with him. He thought he saw the blurred shadow of an old mountain woman, but as she got closer, he could see that she had an enormous mouth that stretched from ear to ear. Her hair was flying wildly around her head, and her eyes seemed to be filled with glowing charcoals.

"This must be the terrible mountain witch," the peddler thought fearfully. "I never thought such a creature really lived!"

He turned around and looked again. The old witch had a horrible face. The peddler shivered and walked faster and faster, but still he could hear her footsteps plodding along behind him. Now the peddler began to run, but as he ran, the witch ran with him. The faster he went, the faster she seemed to follow.

Finally, she called out to him in a strange, crackling voice, "Say, Mr. Peddler, give me your salted mackerel. I'm terribly hungry!"

The peddler hurried on, pretending not to hear, but

soon she shouted again. "Give me your mackerel!" she shrieked. "I want your salt mackerel!"

"I can't let you have any," the peddler shouted back. "I'm taking them to the village to sell!" And he ran on and on, trying to keep ahead of her.

"Very well, Mr. Peddler," the witch called. "If you won't give me your mackerel, I'll eat you and your horse too!"

This time when the peddler looked back, the witch had very nearly caught up with him. He could see her sharp pointed teeth and her wild hair blowing over her hideous face. The poor peddler was so frightened, he dropped the reins of his horse, left behind all his precious mackerel, and ran as fast as he could into the woods.

"Help! Help!" he shouted, but his voice drifted away into the silent night. The woods were dark and cold, and the branches of the trees seemed to swoop down around him like hundreds of mountain witches.

"If only I could find a place to spend the night," the peddler thought as he ran on in the darkness.

Suddenly, he saw a light in the distance, and he hurried toward it as fast as he could. When he got closer, he saw that the light came from a small wooden house.

"Ah, this must be the home of some woodcutter," he thought happily, and he went to the door to knock.

"Gomen kudasai! Is anybody home?" he called, but

there was no answer. He slid open the door and peered in. *"Gomen kudasai!* Excuse me!" he called, but still no one came to welcome him in from the night. No one offered to give him a cup of tea. But the peddler was too tired to care. He decided to go in, and taking off his straw sandals, he tiptoed into the little house. He climbed up the steep steps to the second floor and still there was no one. The peddler stretched out on the *tatami* and closed his eyes. "How good it is to rest," he thought, and trying to forget the terrible mountain witch, he soon fell asleep.

Toward midnight, the peddler suddenly woke up and heard a voice downstairs. "The woodcutter has come home," he thought sleepily, and rubbing his eyes, he started toward the steps. But as he listened carefully, he didn't hear the sound of a woodcutter's voice at all. It was the voice of an old woman.

"My, what a good dinner that was!" the voice said happily. "Two barrels of salt mackerel and a horse to go with them!"

The poor peddler suddenly realized where he was. This was no woodcutter's home at all. It was the house of the mountain witch herself! He was so frightened, he didn't know what to do. If he went downstairs now, he would surely be eaten up.

"I'll have to wait quietly up here until she goes to

sleep," he thought. "Once she is asleep, I will slip out quietly."

And so the peddler crouched at the top of the steps waiting to see what she would do.

Soon the witch began to talk to herself. "Shall I have some tea now, or shall I eat a rice cake?" she murmured.

Now the peddler was so hungry, the thought of a rice cake was delicious. "Have the rice cake," he muttered softly. "Have the rice cake!"

The old witch didn't seem to find it at all strange to hear someone answer her. "Very well," she said then. "I shall have the rice cake."

She put some charcoals into the brazier and then left three rice cakes on top of a grill to toast. The wonderful warm smell of toasted rice cakes filled the room and drifted up to the peddler sitting beside the steps. He was so hungry now, the thought of the rice cakes made his head swim.

"I simply must have one of those rice cakes," he thought, and he waited patiently for the witch to leave the room.

When she finally got up to get some soy sauce, the peddler speared the rice cakes with a long pole and quickly gobbled them up before the witch got back. When she returned, she found only the red coals blinking at her from the brazier.

"Why, what has happened to my rice cakes?" she said, and she looked everywhere in the room, but there was not a trace of them anywhere.

"Those miserable mice must have eaten them," she said at last, and still she did not know that the peddler was hiding right over her head.

"Well, if I can't eat rice cake, I shall go to sleep," she said with a great yawn. "Shall I sleep upstairs on the quilt or downstairs inside the nice warm kettle?"

"It will never do to have her come upstairs now," the peddler thought. Quickly he whispered, "Sleep downstairs in the kettle. Downstairs in the kettle!"

The witch answered sleepily, "Very well, very well, I'll sleep downstairs in the kettle," and she climbed into the big kettle and closed her eyes.

The peddler waited until her breathing was heavy with sleep, then, slowly, slowly, he tiptoed down the steps.

"Now, I shall capture the old witch," he thought, and softly, softly, he put the big wooden lid on top of the kettle. Then, he found a heavy stone and put it on top so the witch could not get out. He put some kindling beneath the kettle and struck a flint to light the fire. The sparks flew everywhere and soon the flames began to spit and crackle.

Inside the kettle, the old witch heard the sound of the

fire, and stirring in her sleep, she murmured, "My, the birds are twittering early."

Before long, the fire blazed beneath the kettle. The old witch felt warm and cozy, and the roar of the fire sounded like the wind in the trees.

"Ha ha!" she laughed. "The wind sweeps through the forest, but I am warm and full of good food. Tomorrow I shall go out and steal more fish from some frightened peddler!" And still she did not know what was happening beneath the pot.

When the fire was burning well, the peddler ran out of the house. "You'll steal no more, old witch," he shouted, and as he ran, he could hear her roaring angrily inside the pot.

"Who shut me inside my own kettle?" she shouted. "Let me out! Let me out!"

But the peddler remembered how she had eaten his horse and all his mackerel. He thought of the other lonely travelers she would frighten if he let her out, and so he turned away quickly and ran back to his own village over the hill.

When he got home, he told the people of his village how he had captured the old witch of the mountains alone. "She will never bother anyone again," he said.

And they answered saying, "You are a brave man!

How good it will be to walk through the mountain forest and not be afraid."

There was much rejoicing in the village and the people brought gifts of rice and wine and gold to thank the peddler for what he had done. He became a man much respected in the little seaside village, and soon became so prosperous he never had to go out to sell salt mackerel again.

The Man
Who Bought a Dream

Once upon a time, there lived a young man who sold
silk cloth and colored thread. He carried them in a big
bundle on his back and went from one village to another
selling his wares.

One day, when he was going to a mountain village beside the sea, he met an old man who was traveling the
same road.

"It is good to have someone to walk with," the young
man said, and the two of them followed the path beside
the sea. The summer day was warm, but a cool breeze
drifted in from the water and made the trees rustle gently
over their heads.

As they walked along, however, the sun grew hot and
the breeze died away. The old man walked slowly, and
still more slowly, until soon he sighed, "How sleepy this
sun has made me. If I could just rest for a moment."

"Then take a nap, old man," the young man answered. "We have time and I can wait."

And so the two men put down their bundles and sat beneath a pine tree growing in the white sand. The old man stretched out in the shade and was soon fast asleep, for he was tired from the long walk. The young man sat beside him, and watched as the old man's face relaxed in sleep. All his wrinkles seemed to fall away as he slept. Suddenly, the young man saw something very strange. A bee climbed out of the old man's ear and then flew out over the water.

"This is most peculiar," the young man thought to himself. "How did the bee ever get into the old man's ear."

As he sat wondering, the bee came back, circled over the old man's face twice, and then flew up into the sky.

"Now what could this mean?" the young man thought to himself, and he sat silently, gazing in wonder at the old man's face.

Before long, the old man awoke. He stretched and yawned a great wide yawn, and then said sleepily, "My, that was an interesting dream!"

"Ah, so you had a dream," the young man said. "Did you dream that a bee climbed into your ear and stung you?"

"No," the old man answered. "But there was surely a

bee in my dream. It flew to me from that island beyond, and told me many things. It told me that there was a white camellia tree on that island, and that if I dug at its roots, I would find a box of gold."

"And, in your dream, did you find the gold?" the young man asked.

"Yes, yes," the old man answered. "I dreamed that I rowed out to the island and found a camellia tree full of white blossoms. I found a box of gold at its roots and became the wealthiest man in all the land. Now, wasn't that a fine dream?"

"Indeed it was, old man," the young man answered. "But tell me, how did you know where to find the camellia tree?"

"Ah, the bee also told me that," said the old man. "It told me the tree would be blooming on a hill just behind the land of the wealthy lord who lives on the island. And when I went to look, that was surely where the camellia tree stood."

Suddenly, the young man turned to him and said, "Look, old man, I'd like to buy that dream from you."

The old man shook his head and laughed. "Now surely, that is the strangest request I have ever heard. There is no need for you to buy it from me, for I have already told it to you, so it is also yours."

But the young man would not listen. "No, no, it is not

really mine until I buy it from you," he said, and he begged the man to sell it to him.

"Well, if you really want to buy it so badly," said the old man, "of course, I shall sell it to you."

The young man took three gold coins from his bag and gave them to the old man. "Now," he said happily, "the dream has become mine."

The two men walked the mountain path to the village, and then they parted and went their separate ways.

"I hope you enjoy my dream," the old man called out as he left.

"I will, old man, I will," the young man answered, and he headed down the village road to sell his cloth and thread.

When he had sold all that was in his bundle, he hurried home to his own village. On the way back, he walked the same path he had taken with the old man. He looked toward the sea and saw the dim outlines of the island edging out over the water. He thought of the dream he had bought, and could not forget the bee that had circled over the old man's head.

"I wonder," the young man murmured to himself. "I wonder if it is really so," and he decided he could not rest until he went to the island to find out.

The very next day, he packed his things in a bundle, and set out over the water in a small rowboat. As he got closer and closer, he saw that it was a lovely little island, full of green trees and low hills that dipped up and down over the land.

"I know I shall find that camellia tree somewhere," he thought to himself, and he headed for the estate of the great lord who lived on the highest hill. "I shall ask this lord if I can work for him," the young man thought, "then I shall be able to look for the tree that grows behind his land."

He knocked at the gate of the lord's estate and said, "I've come from across the water, and would like to find some work. I ask only for food and a place to stay in return."

"Well, now! You are a timely arrival," the lord said. "I was just looking for a man to sweep my walk and trim the leaves of my pine. Can you do these things?"

The young man bowed low. "I can sweep and I can also tend a garden. I should be most grateful if you could use me."

"Good! You are hired," said the lord.

And so it was decided the young man would live in the house of the lord and take care of his garden in return. He got up early in the morning, and worked hard all day. He worked through the fall and the long cold winter, waiting patiently for spring when the camellia trees would bloom.

At last, as the snow began to melt away and the smell of spring filled the air, the young man began to roam the hills behind the lord's estate. He wandered up and down the hills, stopping to look at every tree with a blossom. Sometimes he would see white blossoms and rush to look, only to find that they were not camellias at all. Sometimes, he would see the dark shiny leaves of a camellia tree, but the blossoms would be as red as the sunset itself.

"Perhaps I was foolish to believe in that dream," the young man thought sadly.

Before long, the camellia trees became flowerless, and the air began to grow cold and chill. The hills turned scarlet and gold, and once again, autumn had come to the small island.

"I shall wait for next spring," the young man thought, and he worked hard each day, thinking of the long year that must pass.

At last, when the air grew warm and the trees became tipped with faint green again, the young man went out once more to look for his white camellia tree.

"I must surely find it this spring, or I shall give up and return home," he thought forlornly.

One morning, he got up very early and set off for the hills before working in the garden. He climbed the farthest hill and roamed deep into a ravine where once a river had run. As he peered among the trees, he suddenly saw the dark green leaves of a camellia tree glistening in the sun. And among the leaves were blossoms with smooth petals, like tufts of white snow.

"At last! There it is!" the young man shouted happily, and pulling out his shovel, he began to dig at the root of the tree. He dug and he dug, and finally, his shovel struck something hard.

Clink . . . clank . . . CLINK . . . CLANK . . . The shovel struck it again and again. The young man got on his knees and pushed the dirt away. There, at the bottom of the hole was a wooden box. He opened it with trembling hands and found it filled with golden coins, just as it had been in the dream.

"At last, after two long years," the young man sighed, and he carried the box home to his room, thinking of the bee and the old man who had sold him the dream. When he counted the gold, there was enough for him to live exactly as the wealthy lord in whose home he was working.

The very next day, he went to the lord saying, "Sir, I have been here for two years, and now would like to return home. Please give me permission to leave."

The great lord nodded his head. "You have worked hard and faithfully," he said, and giving him many gifts, he sent the young man on his way home.

The young man went home laden with gold and gifts, and soon became the wealthiest man in all the village. He built a great mansion on top of a hill, where he could look out over the sea. Sometimes, when the sky was blue and the air was clear, he could see the little island looming out of the water and would remember the white camellia tree he had found on the farthest hill. On those days, the young man would smile and murmur to himself, "It was a fine dream! A very fine dream indeed!"

The Fox and the Bear

Long ago, deep, deep in the hills of Japan, there lived a fox and a bear. Neither of them had been able to find much food and both of them were very hungry, so one day the fox came to the bear with a plan.

"I have a good idea, Mr. Bear," the fox said. "Will you listen?"

"Yes, of course," answered the bear. "What is this idea of yours?"

"Well, at the edge of this forest there is a great wide field," the fox explained. "There is nothing growing in it now, but it could be full of cabbages and onions and good things to eat."

The bear nodded, but he still did not understand. "How?" he asked.

"Why, we'll put them there," the fox went on. "All we

need to do is till the soil and plant some seeds. Are you willing to do a little work?"

The bear thought of juicy red carrots and big heads of sweet cabbage, and he could not refuse. "Of course I'll work," he said. "Let's begin right away."

And so the two of them went off to inspect the great wide field at the edge of the forest. It was full of rocks and weeds that needed to be taken out before anything could be planted.

"Mr. Bear," the fox said as he looked at the land. "You are so much stronger than I, and you have much sharper claws. Will you dig up the land and clear the field while I go home and get some seed?"

So, while the fox went home, the bear got to work. He dug up the tree stumps that were in the middle of the field. He cleared away all the big rocks and he plowed the field in neat, straight rows. When at last he was finished, the fox appeared carrying a big bag of seed.

"Ah, you have done a fine job, Mr. Bear," he said, looking over the freshly turned soil. "Now, I shall begin my work."

And the fox trotted back and forth, dropping seeds into the soil. Every once in a while, he would stop to rest beneath the shade of a tree saying, "My, this is difficult!" and he would look at the bear to make sure he understood how hard he was working.

When he had finished, he sat down beside the bear. "Well, our planting is done," he said. "Now, all we have to do is wait for the crops to grow. Let's decide who is going to get which half of the crop, so we won't quarrel about it later," the fox suggested.

"All right," the bear agreed. "That's a good idea."

But before he could say anything more, the fox quickly added, "I'll take the half that grows under the soil."

There was nothing left for the bear to say then except, "Very well, I'll take the half that grows on top of the soil."

And so the two agreed to meet again in a few weeks when their crops would be ready to pick, and each went back to his home in the woods.

Before long, tiny green shoots began to appear in even rows over the field, growing bigger and stronger as the days went by. Finally, one day, the fox and the bear decided it was time to harvest their crops and have a feast.

"Look, Mr. Bear," the fox said cheerfully. "You're going to get all that lovely green that's growing on top of the soil."

The bear nodded happily, and lumbered out into the field to pick his half of the crop. As he began to work, the fox called out to him. "Say, Mr. Bear, since you're picking the greens anyway, pull out the roots for me at the same time, will you?"

The bear was so glad to see all the greens, he didn't even mind helping the fox with his half of the crop. While the bear was busy pulling up the crop, the fox was busy cutting off the roots for himself. Soon, he had filled his own baskets full and slipped away quietly. The bear gathered his green leaves in many bundles and then carried them to his cave.

But the next morning, when the bear got up and looked at his greens, he found they had already begun to wither and dry. He tried eating a few, but they were bitter and tasteless.

"I wonder how the fox made out," the bear thought to himself, and he hurried through the forest to visit the fox.

When he got to the fox's home, he saw him lying in the sun, nibbling on a tender juicy carrot. When he looked inside, he saw that the fox had stored away many, many baskets all full of tender sweet carrots.

"Were those the roots I dug up for you yesterday?" the bear asked in surprise.

"Why, yes, Mr. Bear," the fox answered without even looking up. "How were your greens?"

"They have already begun to dry, and I couldn't even eat any this morning," the bear said forlornly. Then, looking at all the carrots the fox had, he asked, "Let me have a few of your carrots, Mr. Fox."

But the fox shook his head. "Remember, we made a bargain at the very beginning. You were to get everything that grew on top of the soil, and I was to get everything underneath. A promise is a promise." And the fox wouldn't even give the hungry bear one nibble of his carrot.

A few weeks later, just when the bear had begun to forget about the clever fox, he appeared again in front of the bear's cave.

"I admit I wasn't very fair the last time," he said. "Let's plant another crop, and this time you can choose first which half of the crop you'd like."

The bear wasn't going to be fooled again. "Very well," he said. "This time, I want the half that grows beneath the soil. You take what grows on top."

"Anything you say," the fox answered, and again he trotted away to get the seeds while the bear plowed and dug up the field.

After a few weeks, the bear and the fox met again to look at their crops and found rows and rows of beautiful green leaves.

"Now, Mr. Fox, you take what's on top," the bear said, "and I'll take what's under the ground."

The fox nodded, and quickly got to work picking his crop. When his arms were full, he went home, calling to the bear, "Everything underneath is yours, Mr. Bear."

But when the bear dug up the roots, expecting to find nice tender carrots, all he found were a few thin, scraggly roots about an inch long.

"Why, these aren't carrots!" he thought angrily. "I can't even eat these tiny roots," and he ran to see what the fox had taken home. There he found the fox with several baskets full of beautiful red strawberries. He sat eating them one by one, looking up every once in a while to see if the bear was coming.

"Mr. Fox, you've tricked me again," the bear cried angrily. "Let me at least taste one of your strawberries!"

But the fox shook his head. "You chose the bottom half. You can't have any of the top." And so the bear wandered off sad and hungry.

The bear decided then and there that he would have nothing more to do with the sly fox, but one day the fox appeared again.

"I have been very wicked," he said, looking very humble. "But let's forget the past and be friends once more. I came today to show you something I know you'll like. Will you come with me?"

"What is it?" the bear asked, for he was going to be very careful this time.

"I've found a beehive full of honey," said the fox, "and I hurried here to tell you because I know how much you like it."

The Fox and the Bear

When the bear thought of eating some honey, he could not stay away. He followed the fox into a bamboo thicket where the fox pointed out a beehive in the stump of an old tree.

The bear thought of the sweet, creamy honey inside, and said happily, "Ah, that is truly what I love best." He thanked the fox, and then hurried to the beehive, sniffing all around it to see how he could get the honey. But suddenly, the bees came swarming out of the hive, and buzzing wildly, they stung the poor bear and chased him all the way over the hill, back to his cave in the mountains. The clever fox waited quietly until all the bees had gone after the bear, then he went to the beehive and ate all the honey by himself.

This time the bear really lost his patience. "This is the last time that fox will fool me," he said. "I am going to get my revenge." And he wondered what he might do to punish the wicked fox.

One day, as the bear was eating some horse meat, the fox came strolling up to him. "Good day, Mr. Bear," he said, bowing low. "My, that looks like a good piece of meat. May I have just a little taste?"

The bear suddenly had a good plan. "Go right ahead," he said to the fox. "Take as much as you like."

The fox ate until he was full, and then with a happy

sigh, he asked, "Where did you ever find such good horse meat?"

The bear smiled to himself. "It's really very easy, especially for someone your size," he said to the fox.

The fox thought of all the horse meat he could store up for the winter. "Tell me," he said anxiously. "Where do I go? What do I do?"

"Well," the bear went on, "I discovered that just beyond this mountain is a wide meadow beside a cool stream. The meadow is full of green grass, and you will see many, many horses grazing there."

"Yes, yes," the fox said, listening carefully.

"Pick out the biggest horse—the very biggest one you see in the field," the bear went on. "Tie your tail securely to his, and then bite one of his hind legs as hard as you can."

"Is that all?" asked the fox.

The bear nodded. "As soon as you bite the horse's leg, he will weaken and die. Then you'll have all the horse meat you can eat."

The fox hardly waited to thank the bear. He ran as quickly as he could to the big meadow beside the mountain stream. It was green and lovely, and there were many horses grazing there, just as the bear had said. The fox stole quietly behind a big white horse and tied his own tail securely to the horse's. Then he bit one of the hind legs just as hard as he could. The horse gave a terrible cry, kicked up his hind legs, and ran wildly over the field, dragging the fox behind him.

"Help! Stop!" the fox shouted, but the frightened horse just ran all the more. The fox was kicked and dragged over all the stones and stumps that lay in the meadow, and finally thrown against a big tree beside the stream. He was sitting there holding his aching head and moaning to himself when the bear came along to see what had happened.

"Look at me!" the fox whimpered, licking his wounds. "Look what that terrible horse did to me!"

But the bear didn't feel a bit sorry for the fox. "Mr. Fox," he said quietly, "you got exactly what you deserved." And he walked away into the forest without even looking back.

The Tiny God

One day, long, long ago, Prince Okuninushi was walking along the shores of the Japan Sea. As he watched the white foam sparkle over the water, he suddenly saw a tiny speck floating toward the shore. It came closer and closer, and soon the Prince saw that it was a small boat, made from the leaf of a sweet potato. And on top of the leaf sat a tiny man, about the size of his little finger. The leaf drifted to the beach on the crest of a wave, and the little man hopped off, stretched his arms, and looked around.

"Well! What's this?" said the Prince, and he picked up the little man and put him on the palm of his hand. "Ha, ha! A one-inch lad!" he laughed, pinching the little man's nose. "Tell me, where did you come from?"

But the little man scowled and would not answer. Instead, he jumped up and bit the Prince on the cheek.

"Ouch!" cried the Prince. "I'm sorry to have made fun of you. I promise not to pinch your nose any more, so please tell me who you are."

But still the little man looked glumly toward the sea, and refused to open his mouth.

The Prince turned to a crooked pine that stood bent and doubled with age. "Pine tree, do you know this little man?" he asked.

The pine tree waved its green branches gently. "Noooooo, noooooo, I don't know who he is," it answered solemnly.

The Prince saw a sparrow perched on the branch of the pine tree. "Tell me, good sparrow, do you know this little man?"

But the sparrow chirped noisily, "Don't know, don't know, don't know!"

At the foot of the pine tree sat a big fat frog. "Mr. Frog," the Prince said. "Who is this little man? Do you know him at all?"

But the frog blinked his big bulging eyes and answered, "Garrumph! I don't know. Garrumph! I don't know."

As the Prince was about to turn away, the frog added, "Ask the scarecrow in the field. He knows everything."

So the Prince hurried to the scarecrow that stood in the rice field. "Mr. Scarecrow," he said. "The frog tells me you know everything. Can you tell me who this little man is?"

"Why, of course I can," the scarecrow answered. "I know everything. That little man is a tiny god from the land across the sea."

"A god!" exclaimed the Prince, and he looked again at the small glum man in the palm of his hand. "He hardly looks like a god," the Prince thought to himself. "But if the scarecrow says so, then he must be a god." And he bowed to the god saying, "Forgive me for calling you a one-inch lad and for pinching your nose. I did not know you were a god."

When the Prince said that, the tiny god smiled for the first time. "I shall teach you many things, and will help the people of your land to become prosperous and happy," he said. "But first, let me see how much patience and endurance you have."

The Prince smiled. "Certainly," he said. "I'll do anything you say."

"Good!" said the tiny god. "Then let us have a match to see who has more endurance, you or I."

The Prince looked down at the tiny god. "But I am so much bigger and so much stronger, it does not seem quite fair," he said.

But the tiny god only laughed. "Size doesn't make a bit of difference," he said. "Now tell me which you think is harder, to be one-legged like the scarecrow, or to carry a heavy pack on your back?"

"Why, it would be much harder to carry a heavy pack," the Prince said.

"Very well then," answered the god. "I shall take the harder task. I shall carry a heavy pack on my back, and you hop on one foot like the scarecrow. Then let us head for the mountain over there, and see who can keep going the longest."

"That's easy!" said the Prince. "It is nothing to hop on one foot, if I do not have a heavy pack to carry." And he watched with a smile as the tiny god filled a sack full of dirt and hoisted it on his back.

"Are you ready?" asked the god.

"Ready!" answered the Prince, hopping on one foot.

And the two set off down the narrow dirt path toward the foot of the distant mountain. The sky was bright and clear, and the sun shone down through the branches of the trees. The Prince hopped along down the path, getting far ahead of the tiny god who plodded along with the heavy pack on his shoulders.

The Prince looked back at the tiny god, and called, "Are you all right? Isn't your pack getting heavy?"

The tiny god was puffing, but he called back in a loud strong voice, "Don't worry about me. I'm quite all right!"

So the two went on and on, the Prince hopping on one

foot, and the little god walking slowly, with his head bent down. Gradually, the Prince began to feel terribly tired. The foot he held in his hand grew heavy and cramped, and there were many stones in the road that got in his way. He began to hop slowly, and more slowly, and still more s-l-o-w-l-y, until soon he was hardly moving at all.

"Oh, if I could just rest for a minute and stretch my leg!" he thought. But when he looked back, he could see the tiny god catching up with him. "I can't stop now!" he thought, and he continued to hop . . . hop . . . hop. Soon the tiny god was walking right at his heel.

"Getting tired?" asked the little god. "Want to give up?"

But the Prince shook his head. He was too tired to even open his mouth. Finally, when they came to the foot of a big tree, the Prince could go no further. "I give up!" he shouted, and he stumbled to the shade of the tree, stretching out his tired legs.

The tiny god put down his pack, and breathing heavily, he sat down beside the Prince. "I guess I won," he gasped.

The two of them looked at each other. They were both hot and tired and puffing so hard, they could hardly talk. They looked at each other's dusty dirty faces, and suddenly burst out laughing. And from that moment on, the tiny god and the Prince became good friends.

"You lost, but you did well," said the tiny god. "I

shall teach you many things, and your land and your people will prosper."

From that day on, the Prince and the god went everywhere together. The tiny god taught the Prince how to get silk from the cocoon of the silkworm. He told him about medicines and herbs that would heal the sick, and showed him how a marsh could be made into a fertile field. He taught him how to till the soil and plant the crops, and showed him how wheat should be planted after the rice was harvested from the fields. And as the Prince learned these things, he in turn taught them to the people of his land, so they soon became healthy and strong, and raised many fine crops.

At last one day, the tiny god came to the Prince and said, "The time has come for me to say good-bye."

"But why?" asked the Prince sadly, for he had come to love the little god dearly. "We have such good times together, and there is still so much I want to learn."

But the tiny god shook his head. "I have taught you everything I know," he said. "Your land is prospering and your people are happy. It is time for me to go to another land."

The Prince tried to think of reasons why the god shouldn't go. "Your boat has been washed away," he said. "There is no way for you to leave my land."

But the tiny god laughed. "There are many other

118

ways," he said. "I am small and I am light. It will be quite simple for me to leave."

"Ah," said the Prince. "You will jump on the back of a swallow and fly over the seas with him."

The tiny god smiled again. "No, no, that's not it," he said.

The Prince looked around. He looked up at the sky and saw a white cloud drifting lazily over the pines. "You will hop on that cloud and drift away?"

"No. Still no," answered the god.

"Then you will float away with the north wind that sweeps out over the sea," said the Prince.

But the tiny god shook his head. "Come with me, and I will show you," he said, and he led the Prince to a field of golden grain that glistened in the sun. "This is how I shall leave," he said, pointing to the grain.

"But how?" asked the Prince. "Grain does not move. Its roots grow deep and far into the ground."

"Watch!" said the tiny god, and he grasped one of the stalks and climbed to the top. There he bobbed up and down, and the weight of his body made the stalk sway as if a great breeze had suddenly come along.

"It's time to say good-bye now," the tiny god said. And as the stalk of grain swung more and more, he suddenly sprang into the air and flew high into the sky. As he climbed up toward the sun, the tiny god waved to the Prince below.

"Good-bye, dear Prince, *sayonara!*" he called. "Don't forget me!"

The Prince waved back calling, "*Sayonara, sayonara,* come back again some day!" And he watched until the tiny god disappeared into the vast blueness of the sky.

When the little god was gone, the Prince felt sad and lonely, for there was no one with whom he could laugh and talk. Each morning, he went to the seashore to look out over the water, hoping the little god might come back once more.

"Have you seen the little leaf boat today?" he would ask the pine tree, and each day the tree would sigh and whisper, "Not today, my Prince, not today."

One day, as the Prince sat on the beach looking out at the gray mist over the sea, he saw a boat coming slowly toward the shore. But it wasn't the leaf boat, and the man in it was not the tiny god. When the boat reached the shore, a stranger climbed out and walked toward the Prince. "Are you the young Prince that waits each day for the little god?" he asked.

The Prince nodded. "How did you know?" he asked.

The man smiled slowly. "I am a messenger from your friend, the little god," he said. "He asked me to tell you he will not be back, for he has many things to do in

120

other lands. He wants you to know he still thinks of you, but he wants you to work for your people, and not spend your days waiting for him."

The Prince hung his head, and thought how he had not done anything for his people since the tiny god left.

"Return to the little god," he said, "and tell him I shall remember him always. Tell him I will no longer wait for him, and that I will work hard for my people as he taught me to do."

"Ah, that is good," murmured the stranger. "That is what I hoped you would say. Now I can return and tell the tiny god there is no need to worry about you."

Then the messenger climbed back into his boat and headed out toward the sea. "Farewell, young Prince," he called.

Soon the creak of the oars grew further and further away, and the Prince heard only the soft lapping of the waves on the shore.

"Good-bye, friend," he called out into the mist. "And good-bye, little god!" he said.

Then he turned back to go to his palace and to the people of his land.

The Rice Cake
That Rolled Away

Long ago, in a small village in Japan, there once lived a kind old man and woman. One day, they decided they would make some rice cakes, and so the old woman made them and asked the old man to help her fill them with sweet bean paste.

It was a warm day and the sun felt good. "I think I'll take my work outside," the old man said, and he went out to the porch to work in the sun. He sat down on a little cushion, crossed his legs, and set to work. Suddenly, one of the rice cakes rolled off the plate and fell to the ground.

"*Yare, yare,*" the old main exclaimed, and he leaned over to pick it up. But just as he bent down, the rice cake began to roll away down the garden path.

"*Kora, kora!* Stop!" he shouted, but the rice cake rolled on and on.

The old man jumped off the porch, put on his wooden clogs, and ran after the rice cake.

"Where are you going in such a hurry?" he shouted as he ran.

"I'm going as far as the Ojizo-sama's shrine," the rice cake called back. It wouldn't slow down, and it wouldn't stop. It just rolled faster than ever.

The old man ran as fast as he could, but he couldn't catch up with it. Just as he got to the Ojizo-sama's shrine, he saw it disappear into a little hole. The old man peered down into the dark hole, but he couldn't see a thing. He poked his toe into the hole and found that it was much bigger than it seemed from the outside.

"Well, I guess I'll just have to crawl in after that rice cake," the old man thought to himself, and he squeezed his way into the hole. When he got inside, he found to his surprise that it was quite large and roomy.

The old man blinked and brushed the dirt from his clothes, and when he looked up he found that he was standing right in front of the stone statue of Ojizo-sama.

"Ah, forgive me, Ojizo-sama," he said, bowing low. "I did not know I would find you here. I simply came after this stupid rice cake which rolled away from my front porch."

Then the old man picked up his rice cake and broke

it in two. He gave the clean half to the Ojizo-sama and kept the half covered with dirt for himself.

"Please accept my humble gift," he said, "even though it is only half a rice cake."

The statue took the rice cake, and then suddenly, in a low voice that sounded like the rumbling of the waves of the ocean, he spoke to the old man.

"Climb up on my lap," he said.

But the old man was sure he had not heard correctly. He cupped his hand behind his ear and said, "I beg your pardon, but I am old and a little deaf. What did you just say to me?"

The Ojizo-sama smiled. "I said climb up on my lap, old man," he repeated.

This time the old man knew he had heard quite clearly, but he couldn't think of climbing on the lap of the god.

"Oh no, sir. I could not possibly climb up on your lap," the old man said. "That would be most disrespectful."

But the god would not listen. "Do as I say, old man," he said.

And so the old man finally took off his clogs and climbed up on the god's lap. As soon as he did, the god spoke again. "Now, old man, get up on my shoulders!"

The old man shuddered. "Oh, never, never!" he said. "Why that would be a terrible thing to do."

But the Ojizo-sama insisted. "You are a stubborn old man," he said. "Do as I say."

And so the old man climbed up to the shoulder of the stone god. Then he spoke once more. "Now, old man, quickly—up on my head!"

The old man knew it was no use to refuse, so he simply did as he was told. When he had climbed on the god's head, the god handed him a fan.

"Listen carefully, old man," he said. "Very soon a group of ogres will come to gamble and drink in front of me. When they have played a while, beat the fan and crow like a cock."

Now that seemed a very strange thing to do, but the old man listened carefully, and waited to do as he was told. Soon he heard the sound of laughter, and a crowd of ogres with horrible, ugly faces gathered in front of the statue. They rolled out dice, and took out great piles of gold which they spread on the ground. They laughed and they shouted, and they made terrible ogre-like noises that echoed and re-echoed in the emptiness of the deep hole. After a while, the old man decided it was time to do as the god had told him. He beat his fan several times, and then he crowed like a cock.

"Cockarooka-roo! Cockarooka-roo!" he shouted at the top of his voice.

The Rice Cake That Rolled Away

When the ogres heard him, they suddenly dropped what they were doing.

"What! Is it morning already?" they shouted, and stumbling over each other, they scrambled off into the darkness, leaving behind all their gold. When the old man looked down, he saw golden coins scattered everywhere.

"Now, get down, old man," the god said, "and take all the gold the ogres left behind. It is all yours."

The old man filled two sacks with the gold the ogres had left behind. Then he bowed low to the stone god, saying, "Thank you, Ojizo-sama. You have been most generous and kind."

Then he climbed out of the hole and hurried home. When he got there, his wife was waiting patiently for him.

"Where ever have you been?" she asked. "I looked everywhere for you, but all I could find was a bowl of half-filled rice cakes!"

And so the old man told his wife how the rice cake had rolled away, and how he had followed it down to the Ojizo-sama's shrine.

The old woman's eyes grew big and round as she listened to the old man's story about the ogres and their gold. "*Mah, mah!*" she said, and she shook her head and sighed with wonder.

Then the two of them poured the gold from the sacks

and counted the coins to see how much money they had. Just as they were doing this, the old woman from next door came to borrow some rice. She saw the gold spread out on the floor and rubbed her hands greedily. "My, my, where did you get all this money?" she asked. "What have you done to get so rich?"

And so the honest old man and woman told her exactly what happened.

"And you say it all began when the rice cake dropped to the ground?" she asked. "It is a strange story indeed," she said, and she hurried home to tell her husband about it. "Tomorrow I shall send my husband to the shrine to get some of the ogres' gold," she thought to herself.

Early the next morning, the greedy old man and woman next door sat on their veranda and made rice cakes. The old man waited for one to roll off the plate, but not a single one would move. Finally, he picked one up with his fingers and dropped it to the ground. The rice cake fell with a PLOP, but it stayed right where it was, and did not roll.

"What's the matter with you?" the old man said to the rice cake. "If you're not going to roll, I'll make you roll!" And jumping down from the porch, he began to kick the rice cake along the ground. He scuffled along, kicking and prodding the little rice cake, until finally he had pushed it all the way down the dusty road to the

Ojizo-sama's shrine. Still the rice cake would not roll into the hole, so the old man finally pushed it in, and then climbed in after it.

Down in the hole, he found himself standing before the stone Ojizo-sama. He picked up his rice cake, ate the clean sweet bean paste from the inside, and then offered the dirty outside shell to the god.

Then, without even waiting for the god to ask him, he climbed right up on his lap. He waited a few minutes, but the god did not speak, so he climbed up on his shoulder. But still the statue remained silent, so finally the greedy old man climbed right up on his head, and waited for the ogres to come.

"Ah yes, I need the fan," the old man thought, and he leaned down and snatched it from the god's hand.

Very soon, the ogres gathered once more in front of the statue to gamble and to drink. The greedy old man watched happily as the stacks of gold grew higher and higher. Finally, when he could wait no longer, he beat the fan and crowed like a cock.

The ogres stopped, and looked around in surprise. "What? Morning already?" they shouted, and leaving their money scattered on the ground, they ran pell-mell in all directions. One little ogre was in such a hurry, his long red nose got caught in the branch of a tree.

"Help! Help! Something has grabbed my nose!" he

shouted, and he stamped and kicked and looked so comical, the old man could not keep silent.

"Ha ha ha!" he burst out before he could stop himself.

And immediately, the ogres stopped. "That was the laugh of a human being," they shouted, and forgetting to run away, they began to look for the man whose voice they had just heard.

The old man sat on top of the Ojizo-sama's head and trembled with fear. "Please, don't find me," he whispered, but at last one of the ogres looked up and spotted him.

"There he is! There he is!" they shouted, and they dragged the old man from the statue. "It's not morning at all," they cried angrily. "This man tried to deceive us by crowing like a cock!" And they all pounced on him and beat him with their fists.

"Help! Help! Let me go!" the old man shouted, and at last he got away from the ogres and stumbled out of the hole.

He ran for home just as fast as he could, and didn't even stop once to look back. When he got home, his wife asked anxiously, "How much gold did you bring back? I can hardly wait to count it all."

But the old man held out his empty hands. "I was lucky to come back with my life!" he said, and he told

130

the old woman how the ogres had found him and beat him with their fists.

"This is what comes of being so greedy," the old man said sadly, shaking his head.

And from that day on, he never tried to imitate his good neighbor again.

The Grateful Stork

Once long ago, there lived a kind old man and woman who were very, very poor. Each day the old man went out to cut wood in the forest nearby, and then took bundles of kindling into town to sell. The old man went out even when snow fell or great icicles dangled from the roof, for if he didn't sell any wood, there would be no money for their food.

One cold, snowy day, the old man set out for the village as usual, with a bundle of kindling strapped to his back. Great soft snowflakes were swirling down from the gray sky, making shapeless white heaps everywhere.

"Ah, how nice it would be to be back home," the old man thought with a sigh. But he knew he could not turn back, and he trudged on down the snow-covered road, beating his hands to keep them warm.

Suddenly, he saw something strange in the middle of a field. Great white wings seemed to be fluttering and churning up a flurry of snow.

"What is this?" the old man thought, rubbing his eyes. "It looks like a little snowstorm in the middle of the field."

The old man moved closer, and saw that it was a beautiful white stork that had been caught in a trap. The bird fluttered wildly as it tried to get away, but the more it struggled, the tighter the rope around its leg became.

"Poor frightened bird," said the old man, and even though he was shivering from the cold and anxious to get to town, he stopped to help the stork.

"Here, here," he called gently. "Wait a minute. You're getting all tangled in the rope." And bending down, he loosened the rope around the stork's leg. "Let me untie you quickly, before someone comes along and wants to take you home."

When the rope was undone, the stork beat its great white wings and flew off into the sky. The old man heard it crying into the wind as it soared higher and higher. Then, it circled over the old man's head three times, and flew off toward the mountains.

"Good-bye, stork! Good luck!" the old man called, and he watched until it became a small black speck in the sky. Then, picking up his kindling, he hurried toward the village. It was bitterly cold, but inside the old man felt a warm happy glow. Somehow, the stork seemed to be a good omen, and he felt glad to have helped it get away.

He sold all his kindling in the village and then hurried home to tell the old woman how he had saved a stork that had been caught in a trap.

"You did a good thing, my husband," the old woman said, and the two old people thought of the stork flying home into the hills.

Outside, the snow still fell, piling up all along the sides of the house. "How good it is to be inside on a night like this," the old man said, as he heard the rice sputtering in the kitchen and smelled the good bean soup that bubbled in a pot beside it.

Just then, there was a soft rap-rap-rap at the door.

"Now who could be out on a cold night like this?" the old man thought. But before he could get to the door, he heard a gentle voice calling, *"Gomen kudasai . . . Is anybody home?"*

The old woman hurried to the door. "Who is it?" she called, as she slid open the wooden door. There she saw a white figure covered with snow.

"Come in, come in," the old woman urged. "You must be terribly cold."

"Thank you, yes. It is bitterly cold outside," the

stranger said, and she came in shaking the snow from her shoulders. Then the old man and woman saw that she was a beautiful young girl of about seventeen. Her cheeks and her hands were red from the cold.

"Dear child, where are you going on such a terrible night?" they asked.

"I was going to visit some friends in the next village," the young girl explained. "But it is growing dark and I can no longer follow the road. Will you be good enough to let me sleep here just for tonight?"

"I wish we could help you," the old woman said sadly. "But, alas, we are very poor, and we have no quilts to offer you."

"Oh, but I am young," the girl answered. "I don't need any quilts."

"And we can offer you no more than a bowl of rice and soup for supper," the old man added.

But the young girl just shook her head and laughed. "I shall be happy to eat anything you are going to have," she said. "Please do not worry."

So the old man and woman welcomed the young girl into their home, saying, "Come in, come in. Get warm beside the *hibachi*."

But the young girl went instead to the kitchen where the old woman was preparing supper. "Let me help you," she said, and she worked carefully and quickly. When they had eaten, she got up and washed the dishes before the old woman could tell her to stop.

"You are indeed a good and kind child," the old man and woman said happily, and because they had no children, they wished they could keep her as their own child.

The next morning, the young girl awoke early, and when the old man and woman got up, they found the house swept and the rice bubbling over the charcoals. It was the first time the old woman had had breakfast made for her. "My, you are such a help to me!" she said over and over again.

After breakfast, they looked outside, but snow was still swirling down and had piled so high around the house, they couldn't even open the door.

"Will you let me stay another day?" the young girl asked.

The old man and woman nodded quickly. "Why, of course," they said. "Stay as long as you like. Since you have come, our house seems to be filled with the sunshine of spring."

Each morning, the three of them looked outside, but the roads were still filled with snow, and the young girl could not venture out. Before long, five days had gone by, and still she could not leave. Finally, on the morning of the sixth day, she came before the old man and woman and said, "I have something I would like to ask you."

"Anything, anything," they answered. "We will do anything you ask us to do, for we have come to love you as our own daughter."

Then, bending her head low, the young girl began to speak. "You see, my mother and father have just died. I was on my way to the next village to live with some relatives whom I do not even know. I would so much rather stay here with you. If you will let me be your daughter, I will work hard and be a good and faithful child."

When the old man and woman heard this, they could scarcely believe their good fortune, for they had prayed all these years for a child to comfort them in their old age. The good gods had surely heard their prayer to send them such a sweet and gentle child.

"You have made us happier than we can say," they answered to the young girl. "From this day on, we will love you and care for you as if you were our very own."

And so it was decided that the young girl would stay with them always.

One day, the young girl set up a small wooden loom in the corner of the room, and put a screen around it so no one could look in.

"I would like to weave something," she said to the old man. "Will you buy me some thread the next time you go to the village?"

So the old man bought all sorts of beautiful colored thread and gave it to the young girl.

"Now," she said. "I am going to weave something behind that screen, but no matter what happens, you must not look in while I am weaving."

The old man and woman nodded their heads. "All right, child," they said. "No matter what happens, we will not look behind the screen while you are weaving."

Soon, they could hear the sound of the girl working at the loom. "Click-clack . . . click-clack . . . swish . . . clickety-clack . . ." The young girl worked from morning till night, hardly taking time to eat her meals, and all day the sound of the loom filled the little house. For three days she worked behind the screen, and finally, on the night of the third day, she brought out a beautiful piece of cloth.

"Look, Ojii-san and Obaa-san," she said, holding up the cloth, "this is what I have been weaving behind the screen."

The old man and woman took the cloth beneath the lamp so they could see it more clearly. It was a beautiful piece of brocade with silver and white birds flying everywhere, their wings flecked with sunlight. The two old people stroked the cloth with their hands and gasped at the loveliness of it.

"It is beautiful!" they said over and over again.

"Will you take it to the village tomorrow and sell it for me?" the young girl asked the old man.

"Why, of course, of course," the old man answered, "although it seems almost too beautiful to sell to anyone."

"Never mind," the young girl said. "I want you to buy me more thread with the money you get for it, and I will soon weave you another one even more beautiful."

And so, early the next morning, the old man carried the piece of brocade to the village. "Brocade for sale!" he called, as he walked down the street. "I have a beautiful piece of brocade for sale!"

Just then, the wealthy lord who lived at the top of the hill was riding through the streets. He stopped the chair in which he was riding and leaned out the window.

"Say there, old man," he called. "Let's see the brocade you have for sale."

The old man unfolded the piece of cloth and held it up for the lord to see. The great lord stroked his chin and looked at it carefully.

"Hmmmm," he said. "This is the finest piece of brocade I have seen in a long time. It glistens like a thousand snowflakes in the sun." Then he took out a bag full of gold and handed it to the old man. "Take this," he said. "Your piece of brocade is sold."

The old man hurried home with more thread and all sorts of wonderful presents and good things to eat.

"Look what I've brought home," he called happily, and he emptied all the gold coins still left in the sack. "What a happy day for us," he said, and he told the young girl how the lord had marveled over her beautiful cloth.

The very next morning, the young girl again went behind the screen and began to weave another piece of cloth. For three days the house was filled with the sound of the loom, and again, on the night of the third day, she finished another piece of brocade. The next morning, the old man went to the village and searched out the wealthy lord who lived at the top of the hill.

"I have another piece of brocade," the old man said, spreading out the second piece the girl had woven.

The lord looked at it carefully and exclaimed, "Why, this is even more beautiful than the last one." And without a moment's delay, he handed the old man an even bigger bag of gold.

The old man hurried home, laden with thread and gifts, and again they celebrated their good fortune with all kinds of good things to eat.

When the young girl went behind the screen for the third time to weave still another piece of brocade, the old woman could bear it no longer.

"I must take one little peek to see how she weaves that beautiful cloth," she said, and she got up to look behind the screen.

"But we promised," the old man warned. "We told her we wouldn't look, no matter what happened."

But the old woman wouldn't listen. "Just one look won't hurt," she said, and she stole silently to the corner of the room and looked behind the screen.

She could hardly believe her eyes when she looked, for instead of the young girl she expected to see, she saw a great white stork standing before the loom. It was plucking its own soft white feathers and weaving them into the cloth with its long beak. The old woman saw that the bird had already plucked more than half of its feathers to make the beautiful white cloth.

"Ojii-san! Ojii-san!" she cried, running back to the old man, and she told him what she had seen behind the screen.

The old man shook his head sadly. "I told you not to look," he said. And the two old people sat silently, wondering about the strange sight the old woman had seen.

That night, the young girl came out from behind the screen carrying another beautiful piece of brocade. She sat before the old man and woman and bowed low.

"Thank you for being so good and kind to me," she

said. "I am the stork the old man once saved in the snowstorm. Do you remember how you freed me from the trap?" she asked.

The old man nodded and the girl went on. "I wanted to repay you for saving my life, and so I decided to become a young girl and bring good fortune to your lives. But now I can no longer stay, for this morning Obaa-san saw me in my true form, and now you know my disguise."

The old woman hung her head. "Please forgive me," she murmured. "I was so anxious to see how you wove your cloth, I broke my promise to you and am very much ashamed."

"Please don't leave," the old man begged, but the young girl shook her head.

"I cannot stay," she said. "But I leave knowing that you will never be poor or hungry again. Good-bye, dear Ojii-san and Obaa-san."

Then she stepped outside and became once more a beautiful white bird. Glistening in the moonlight, she spread her wings out wide and flew high into the sky. Then, circling three times over the old man and woman, she soared off toward the stars and disappeared over the hills.

The old man and woman were lonely without the

sweet young girl they had grown to love, but they remembered her always. And just as she had said, they were never poor or hungry again, and lived happily and comfortably ever after.

Glossary

Furoshiki	foo-roh-shee-kee	A square cloth used to wrap and carry things.
Gomen kudasai	goh-men koo-dah-sah-ee	"Excuse me"—usually called at the front entrance when visiting someone.
Hibachi	hee-bah-chee	A brazier
Kibutsu-sama	Kee-boo-tsu-sah-mah	Wooden Buddha
Kimono	kee-moh-noh	A Japanese dress
Kora-kora	koh-rah, koh-rah	An exclamation like, "Here, here!" or "Hey!"
Mah-mah	mah-mah	"My, my"
Namu ami dabutsu	nah-moo ah-mee dah-boo-tsu	"May Buddha be praised"
Obaa-san	Oh-bah-sahn	Grandmother or old woman
Ojii-san	Oh-jee-sahn	Grandfather or old man

Ojizo-sama	Oh-jee-zoh-sah-mah	The guardian god of children
Okuninushi	Oh-koo-nee-noo-she	A proper name
Sayonara	sah-yo-nara	Good-bye
Susano	Soo-sah-noh	A proper name
Tatami	tah-tah-mee	A woven rush mat laid over the floor
Yare, yare	yah-rei, yah-rei	An exclamation, like "Oh dear"
Yoisho, yoisho dokkoi-sho	yoi-sho, yoi-sho dok-koi-sho	An exclamation when doing heavy work, like "Heave ho!"

Yoshiko Uchida was born in Alameda, California and grew up in Berkeley, the locale of her recent trilogy, *A Jar of Dreams, The Best Bad Thing* and *The Happiest Ending.* She earned her BA with honors from the University of California, Berkeley, and has a Masters in Education from Smith College.

She began writing when she was ten years old, creating small books out of brown wrapping paper in which to write her stories. She is now the author of twenty-five published books for young people and has won many awards for her work, including a Distinguished Service Award from the University of Oregon.

Her published work for adults includes many articles and short stories as well as a novel, *Picture Bride*, and a non-fiction book, *Desert Exile*, which tells of her family's World War II internment experiences when they were among the 120,000 Japanese Americans imprisoned by the US government.

Although many of her earlier books were about Japan and its young people (including three collections of Japanese folk tales, *The Dancing Kettle, The Magic Listening Cap* and *The Sea of Gold*), her recent work focuses on the Japanese American experience in California.

She says of her work, "I hope to give young Asians a sense of their own history, but at the same time, I want to dispel the stereotypic image held by many non-Asians about the Japanese Americans and write about them as real people. I also want to convey the sense of hope and strength of spirit of the first generation Japanese Americans. Beyond that," she adds, "I want to celebrate our common humanity."